*Nancy Herself*

# *Nancy Herself*

By ERICK BERRY

The Goldsmith
Publishing Company
CHICAGO

MANUFACTURED IN THE UNITED STATES OF AMERICA

# CONTENTS

# *Nancy Herself*

CHAPTER I

# "Miss Elizabeth Kent"

THE outside door was ajar. Nancy opened it quietly. No need to disturb Mrs. Laubenheimer; besides, if she stopped to talk there would be even less daylight between now and four o'clock. With a quick glance over her shoulder she tiptoed up the old stairs to the third floor and with eager, shaking hands fitted a key to a lock. Inside, she leaned, laughing, against the closed door.

"Hello!" said Nancy to the little room. The little room, smiling back, made no audible answer.

The ceiling was low, the walls white, the two windows curtainless, facing north, and so shaded by tall maples that the light was good for only a few hours of the day. That was why one had to hurry. She crossed the room, tugged off her hat, and almost with one gesture slipped out of her cotton dress and into an ancient, paint-smeared smock. Now at last she could turn to the picture on the easel by the window. Was it as good—or as bad—as she had remembered it?

Facing her on a table was a bowl, a big blue bowl filled with the flowers she had been painting. They were dying now, but that didn't matter, she could paint today without them. With eyes narrowed to shut out detail, she considered her work. A leading question to mother yesterday had brought out the remark that shadows on larkspur were hot, that is, tending towards the red end of the spectrum. But that was in sunlight. Had she really made the color too cool?

Oh, and before she began to paint she had

one more thing to do, wind and set the alarm clock. Better do that now. From considerable experience Nancy had learned that only its strident summons could rouse her to reality, once she had begun to work, and get her back home in time to avoid embarrassing questions.

With the alarm set for four she turned to her palette, squeezed paint tubes, mixed colors skilfully, and began to paint. This was sheer joy, but it was discouraging, too. The work was a joy, but difficult when your critical faculty so far outdistanced your ability. That was the trouble with being brought up, as Nancy had, with illustrators and art critics all in the same family.

Sometimes she desperately wished that dad had taken up janitoring or street sweeping or some other peaceful and nonintelligent job; that mother had been something less inspiring, and less critical than an honest-to-goodness magazine illustrator. Having a publisher for a father, a man who saw painters and illustrators all day long, and for a mother someone who knew so terribly much about the one thing Nancy wanted to do, wasn't, she felt, quite fair. It made Nancy feel very young and insecure and ignorant. It started her off with an inferiority complex right at the beginning. If she mentioned an art career to dad he smiled tolerantly, addressed her as "infant," suggested she'd better stick to tennis, and basketball; or, if she really wanted to do something serious, she might concentrate on spelling, goodness knew the younger generation didn't know how to spell. As for mother, Nancy just hadn't dared to tell her about her aspirations. Mother was so awfully talented that Nancy's feeble efforts would seem silly to her, Nancy thought gloomily.

Nancy put a dab of alizarin crimson on the

larkspur shadow and stepped back to squint at it. Yes, that helped. But her shapes were wobbly. She'd been wrong to plunge so quickly into color, she should have made a more careful drawing first. Only color was so exciting, it was hard to discipline oneself into proper preparation.

An automobile passed quietly along the narrow country lane. Nancy caught a glimpse of a dark blue small car. That would be dad getting home in time for tea. She laid down her palette and straightened her cramped arms, standing back for another critical view of the painting, then turned to a hook on the wall and took down the little white purse that went with the summer dress.

Inside was a small, worn clipping. No need to read it again. It was a short notice of an exhibition opening August 30 in the art gallery of a city store and solely for art students and others wishing to study art. There was an award for each class of work from landscapes and portraits to still lifes and black-and-white compositions, some of them were money awards, and three were scholarships at the Art Academy. Pinned to the bottom of the clipping was a green slip, a receipt from the store's art department, dated a week ago, and made out to Miss Elizabeth Kent.

Nancy did so want to win a prize, one of the small money prizes would do. She considered that as she returned to work. She didn't want to ask dad for extra money when he'd had all those doctors' bills last winter. Her small allowance hardly paid for paints and brushes, and certainly left nothing over for this little hidey-hole of a studio. Her small birthday check, two months ago, had gone for rent, and if she wanted to keep the place she felt she must find another check somewhere. Mrs. Laubenheimer, widow of dad's old gardener, was a funny old darling and awfully glad to have her come here, rent or no rent, but Nancy felt it was more businesslike, and that the studio was more her own, if she took the room on a purely professional basis. So she was paying a dollar a week for it.

"Brrrrrr!" The alarm clock snarled warning and she hurried to shut it off. "Time to trot home for tea, Miss Elizabeth Kent," she told herself, and sighed. Mother had said they were invited to the Lees for dinner. Rosilee Lee was a darling, older than Nancy, and the only other person who knew about the little studio. She played the piano almost like a professional, so she could understand about this career business. But there wouldn't be much chance to visit with Rosilee for this was a formal dinner with some distinguished guests invited—several people from the city. Nancy sighed again, slipped the gingham dress over her head and fastened the belt.

What fun if she and mother had a garret studio together, if they had nothing to do but just paint and paint. They'd do the exhibitions together, and see their own work hung together "on the line," which meant not skied, not hung in a dark corner. Mother was such a lamb! Nancy wished she dared talk to her about this art business.

And then for a while she forgot about being a poor artist in Paris, because there were buttered crumpets for tea, and blackberry jam with little cream cheeses. And right after that it was time to dress for dinner, in a dress that had grown too small for mother but was perfect for Nancy, quite long and swirly, with stiff little yellow-and-pink daisies embroidered around the belt. She stood for quite five minutes admiring herself in the tall hall mirror, until mother called, "Hurry, Nancy. Your father's waiting."

Dad did look distinguished, with his white hair in a plume across his forehead, and mother always looked so young she was sometimes taken for Nancy's older sister. Tonight, as the car took them through the pleasant spring dusk she said that she'd just received a new serial to illustrate.

"From the *Illustration Review*. It's by Stephen Kent," she told dad.

"His last three books have been excellent, and all best sellers." Dad frowned as he switched into high and they turned into the main road. "I'd give a hundred dollars if his literary agent would steer him my way. More than that; we need a good, steady writer like that on our list, someone who turns out something worth printing every year or so. But I believe he's tied up with a long-term contract with Lutman."

Funny that dad could think Stephen Kent was such a good writer. He had literary style and all that—but now his girls for instance. For a few minutes she played with the idea of going to a vague, nebulous Stephen Kent, some-one rather plump and round, in horn-rimmed glasses, she pictured him, and saying, "Look here, you'd be lucky to get my father to publish your books. He's the very best publisher in the country!" and then coming back to dad with a manuscript under her arm. But that was silly. Business wasn't done that way. . . . Funny, though, about that name, "Kent." Funny that she should have taken it for her own nom de brush, perhaps because mother had illustrated several of his stories and the name had stayed in the back of her mind. But it didn't matter, she'd certainly never meet the man.

"Who are the Lees' other guests tonight, dad?" she asked, "did they tell you?"

Dad grinned at her in the dusk. "Don't know, Toots. A couple of writers, I think. What's one more writer in this publishing world? Question is rhetorical only! Here we are," and he opened the door for mother to get out.

The dinner table was very gay, with a dozen or so guests ranged along its sides, and a high decoration of white roses and blue larkspur in the center. Nancy's attention was all on the larkspur and the effect of the candlelight on that glorious blue, till she remembered her manners and turned to her dinner partner.

He was tall, rather gray, and wore a monocle. She hadn't caught his name during the introductions, but that monocle fascinated her, for she'd never quite believed that people wore them.

"How do you keep it in?" she asked, as the eye behind the glass twinkled humorously.

"Don't—always," and he opened the eye wide. The glass dropped suddenly to the end of its black cord. Nancy gave a little squeak.

"Could anyone wear one? I mean, is it a decoration for bravery or something?"

The owner of the eyeglass put back his head and shouted with laughter. "No, not a decoration, and anyone could wear one. Sometimes women do, in England. Want to try it?"

He slipped it off, and Nancy, dimpling, practiced first with one eye and then with the other. It stayed in the left eye pretty well till she giggled and it dropped again.

"Londoners sometimes call it a Piccadilly window."

"I've been there," said Nancy, carefully returning the loan. "But it rained all the time. I liked the flower women with their funny hats and round, red faces. And dad took me to see the Changing of the Guards like in Christopher

Robin. But," she hastened to explain, "I was very young," lest her remembrances seem too trivial.

"And do you belong with the house, like Miss Rosilee? This is my first visit and I arrived only today, so forgive me for not knowing."

Nancy shook her head. "No. That's my dad down there, next to Mrs. Lee, and the woman with the dimple like mine, only prettier, is mother. She illustrates, and her professional name is Carol Heywood."

"Mmm!" murmured Nancy's neighbor, nibbling an olive. "Yes, I know."

"She just got another serial today, to illustrate. It's by Stephen Kent," volunteered Nancy proudly. The man might be impressed by the name of the author anyway.

He gave her a quick glance. "Do you read the serials your mother illustrates? And are you sure you like this Stephen Kent?"

Nancy considered thoughtfully as she finished her iced soup. "Dad says he'd like to publish him. Of course that means he's good. But——"

"There's something——?" persisted her neighbor.

"Oh, yes. It's his girls I don't like. I think they're old-fashioned. Perhaps Stephen Kent has lived abroad so long he doesn't know that girls aren't so sentimental and sort of floppy, any more. We're more serious, we have to be."

"Come, come! Surely there isn't a serious thought in that curly head of yours, beyond how well you look in the candlelight in that pretty frock."

That, thought Nancy with an inward snort of wrath, just made her sick. Of all the silly ideas! But she fumbled for a tactful way to put it. "I think you, too, have rather lost touch with young people if that's what you think."

She struggled to make the conversation less personal, to hide her inward resentment. "For instance, in that book of Kent's, *Bound East*, in the scene with Celia—— Did you read that?"

The man's eyes crinkled amusedly. "I'm—er—familiar with it. Yes."

"Mmm. Well, where Celia is deserted, you remember? I think the author handled it all too romantically. He'd made Celia quite modern, or at least he'd *said* that Celia was a modern. Then he has her run home, and mope and mope and *mope* . . . till the man comes back into her life again. All piffle, I say," snorted a modern Nancy from the height of her sixteen years.

"You think she'd have done otherwise?" The man was politely skeptical.

"Celia would have gone to work at some interesting job—made something of herself. She certainly wouldn't have bored everyone in sight by being gloomy and dismal and made her family support her," said Nancy. "I liked her up till then. After that I wanted to shake her." Nancy traced the lace doily under her plate with a pointed forefinger. "For instance, Kent had her know a lot about what's-his-name's work."

"George," supplied the man surprisingly.

"George's work," continued Nancy. "He had her a real help to him, in furnishing the houses he built, so that they sold better. That was part of the plot, that she understood about colors and furniture and things like that. Why didn't she, when she broke with him, go into that line on her own, make a name for herself. Then if she really went on liking George after the way he behaved perhaps they might meet again and he'd have a new estimate of her values. Girls are lots more serious nowadays. Rosilee's taking up music professionally, she's going to train choruses, and I have two friends who mean to study law. That's what Celia would have done, not cried her pretty blue eyes out."

"Gray," corrected the man mechanically and still more surprisingly. "By gracious, I think you're right. Thank you for the criticism. Next time I'll look around for a good example of the modern generation, not try to write so much from memory."

Nancy felt herself getting hot. Now she *had* put her foot in it! "Then *you're* Stephen Kent? I'm so sorry." Her voice was small and meek.

Mr. Kent grinned almost apologetically. "I asked for it, so don't worry. And I'm grateful for so impersonal a criticism."

Nancy felt better. "I know. I think all artists need a good criticism now and then. I'd give a heap for a good critic for my own work."

They had reached the ices by now, and Mr.

Kent didn't seem at all bored with so young a partner. He pushed his dish aside and regarded Nancy quizzically. "Don't tell me I've been talking to a fellow craftsman or I'll think you've merely been displaying professional jealousy!"

"Oh, hardly!" she dropped her voice and glanced down the table. "But I've got to confide in you. You see, I've stolen your name." And she went on to explain about the little studio and entering the competition, and having to find a brush name.

"So I took 'Kent.' Perhaps because mother had been talking about you. You see I couldn't use my own. Dad doesn't believe in a girl taking up art just because she 'thinks she can draw.' It just clutters the world with bad art, he thinks, and anyway, he thinks I'm still a baby. But I mean to show him I've got real talent. I'll bet he'll be very much surprised."

"I shouldn't wonder," murmured Mr. Kent.

"And now, you see, if any mail comes here under my name, it might come to you. I couldn't know you'd be visiting here."

"I am honored at the association," he said. And Nancy thought she rather liked old-fashioned manners after all. "Ah, I note the ladies are leaving. Shall I see you later?"

But the older people talked politics after dinner. Nancy stole through the open French window onto the long terrace and found the one that was nearest the piano. Rosilee might spend the remainder of the evening there, if she didn't get her away. Nancy tapped with a fingernail on the pane, and when the piano stopped and Rosilee's amused face peered out between cupped hands, hissed, "Hey, come on out, I want to talk to you."

Rosilee laughed and stepped through the window. "You made quite a hit at dinner, I noted. We invited Mr. Kent to meet his illustrator. He was supposed to sit by your mother but somehow the cards got mixed."

Nancy grinned ruefully and described what had happened. "I put my foot in it! And what'll you do about the mail for Miss Elizabeth Kent?"

"Oh, that's easy. I'll tend to it. Wait, perhaps there's something already." Rosilee whisked off and returned along the dim terrace with an envelope.

"Here's your mail, Miss Kent," she said with a laugh.

Close to one of the lighted windows they examined the contents and learned that Miss Elizabeth Kent and one friend, on presentation of the enclosed card, would be admitted to the exhibitors' private view of the Art Students' Exhibition.

"Rosilee! That looks as if I were hung—I

mean my picture. Oh, darling, it's tomorrow, and my first exhibition."

"What did you send?" asked Rosilee, almost as thrilled as Nancy.

"A still life. Nasturtiums in a glass bowl on a black table. The drawing's a little wobbly, but the color is nice. I worked like a fiend over it. Now how to get into town for this? Can you come with me?"

But Rosilee couldn't, so Nancy decided to make an appointment for a shampoo, and go into town with dad in the morning, then come out alone by the two-o'clock bus. It seemed a bit elaborate, but being a conspirator with a guilty secret was rather fun, much more exciting than just going ahead without planning.

She didn't mention the exhibition to dad, of course; just said good-by as they came out of the bus station. At the store she took the elevator to the seventh floor. Nancy felt like an

Edgar Wallace heroine. It was thus they evaded pursuers and slipped round corners to keep a rendezvous with adventure. Or perhaps she was a poor and hungry little art student, going, with fast beating heart, to see if her treasured canvas, over which she had worked for a year, was "hung on the line." Nancy grinned to herself. Certainly her heart was beating fast enough, her purse as flat as any art student's.

"Art gal'ry, rugs, needlework, embro'dry, men's and boy's clothing," chanted the elevator man. Nancy headed for the gallery.

Goodness, what a lot of aspiring artists in the world! California and Kansas, Texas and Montana, Boston and New Orleans. Not much chance for Elizabeth Kent, with all this competition. These were all black-and-whites, another room beyond held portraits.

Nancy had cut her teeth on a brush handle,

had played with colors and pencils, inks and crayons all her short life, had heard art talk since she could understand English. All this had developed a fair critical ability. She knew good work when she saw it, and there wasn't much of it here.

The portrait room was full of students and their friends. Nancy saw two girls talking with another with red hair, heard one of them say, "Now Henry said. . . ."

That must, thought Nancy with a pang of envy, mean Mr. Henry, head of the illustrators' class at the Art Academy. He often came to the house as a guest of mother and dad. How she'd like to study with him. And there was dad now!

He stood facing the wall, talking to two other men, one of them Mr. Henry himself. Oh, dear, if they should see her! Nancy dodged round a corner of the next room and with the sound of her father's voice growing fainter in her ears loitered along, looking at the landscapes. No, her own work wasn't here. There must be a separate room for the still lifes.

The door at the end gave onto the rug department. If she went out and around she couldn't get back through another door, for she'd given up her ticket. To return through the portrait room meant that she must pass dad and Mr. Henry. She returned, hovering, listening. The voices had gone. Nancy glanced at her watch. This was ridiculous. In twenty minutes she must be at the hairdresser's, three blocks away. But she couldn't leave, could she, without seeing her own picture?

She repassed those muddy gloomy landscapes. Beyond, the men were clustered, backs to her, in consultation over something. Would it be wiser to scuttle through, or be nonchalant? Nancy decided to be nonchalant. Strolling slowly, intent, apparently, on the details of each separate exhibit, she heard her father's voice behind her, saw him, from the corner of her eye turn partly towards her. But she passed that tight place, almost reached the door. . . .

"The still lifes are next," she heard him say, and slipped through ahead of them, drew a sigh of relief, and let herself hurry.

Suppose her painting wasn't here after all! But it was, and given a good place, too. Nancy paused to gaze, wanted to stay longer. That did look like a nice bit of color, and how well that old frame of mother's fitted it.

The four men entered one end of the long room just as Nancy scurried out the other and fled towards the elevator. It wasn't till she was in the bus again, speeding toward home, that she thought about dad and why he was at that exhibition. "Good gracious, I do believe he was judging the show! Yes, of course, he had a list and so did Mr. Henry— Well!" Life was even more complicated than she had thought.

At dinner she tried to lead the conversation around to the afternoon. "What were you doing today, dad?" "Anything interesting today, dad?" Her father threw her an amused glance, but later he did say to mother, "An amusing bunch of drawings today at the exhibition. Half a dozen quite talented things."

"Oh, what were they?" Nancy dashed in breathlessly and to cover up her eagerness. "Were you a judge?"

Yes, he had been on the committee. And changed the subject again. This, thought his child, is more than any mere daughter should be called upon to endure. But dad was back to the point again. "The awards will be in tomorrow night's paper. We had a little disagreement over two of them, one rather striking still life that I thought very good."

The next day was the longest in Nancy's life. Whenever the phone rang, she jumped, and then it was only the hairdresser for mother, or an editor, or some friends, or anybody that wasn't the right person. Should she call Mr. Kent and ask if anything had come in her name? Why didn't Rosilee phone her if there had been a notice? But maybe they didn't let you know if you'd failed, only if you'd won something. Nancy shut her eyes tight and tried to see her nasturtiums on the wall, but all she could remember was those miles and miles of landscapes.

At six the car brought dad from the station. Dad and the evening papers. Nancy, tearing down the steps to take his hat, hovered at his heels like a pleading puppy. But she couldn't think of a reason why she should want the papers; that is, one she could say aloud.

And then mother and dad went in to dinner. Lagging behind Nancy managed to get a paper open, had found the page, had even found the heading, "Awards To Students In Art Exhibition," when dad's voice came from the dining room:

"Come, Toots. We're waiting for you."

Such a bunch of names to wade through, they swam before her eyes. Nancy dropped the paper guiltily, and with a sick feeling that it didn't matter, she wasn't there. All during the soup course she was close to tears. When the phone rang she jumped but sank back.

But it was for her, it *was*. She dropped her napkin, excused herself briefly, and ran.

The voice, however, wasn't Rosilee's. It was a man's. "Miss Nancy Brewster? Stephen Kent speaking. I have a letter for you."

Oh! Oh! Could he open it? Right now? And read it to her? She felt she could stand any disappointment rather than this suspense. There was an amused grunt, the sound of tearing paper, then his voice again.

"Miss Elizabeth Kent. My dear Miss Kent, we take pleasure in informing you. . . ." And so on to the end. Nancy's eyes were like stars.

At the end she said, "Oh . . . Oh!" in a small voice, and "Thank you, that was awfully kind of you."

"Was that what you expected? No? Well, it's good, isn't it?" Oh yes, it was good, and before she could hang up, "Would you carry a message for me?"

With knees that were shaking, because it mattered so very, very much, she returned to the dining room and stood, hands behind her, back of dad's chair. How should she put it? How should she swallow her disappointment, and put up with the little she had gained?

"Dad, you owe me a hundred dollars. Mother heard you say you'd pay it. But if you don't mind, I'd like to swap it for something else."

Dad laughed. "And do I really? And what is the swap for, some new dress?"

Nancy shook her head, and came round to face him. "No, I want to——" she gulped and made the plunge—— "I want to go into town three times a week, all next year, afternoons, starting with October. I'll see that it doesn't interfere with school. I'll need railway fare."

Dad raised his eyebrows. "And for what is the hundred?"

"For a message from Mr. Stephen Kent. He says could he come in and talk over a possible contract with you, for his next novel. That is, on condition that I'll help him when he comes to write his heroine, so she will be Edward the Eighthian and not Victorian. You said—you did say that you'd give a hundred to get him on your next book list."

Mother was smiling and nodding. "She has you there, Jim. I heard you. But why town three times a week, Nancy?"

"I want it to take me into the Art Academy." Nancy knew that her voice was shaking, she cared so terribly about this. And it all hung on one thing. . . .

Mother gave a little chuckle and Nancy knew that she'd won in that quarter. Perhaps mother'd known all along that Nancy wanted to be an artist.

"What's all this nonsense?" asked dad. "You can't draw."

Nancy giggled. "There seemed to be a difference of opinion on that point," she said, "yesterday you weren't so sure!"

"Yesterday?"

Nancy brought out the paper from behind her back. It was folded to the announcement. Her fingers traced. "Judges . . . Mr. John Henry . . . Mr. James Brewster. . . ." And then along to, "The judges were unable to agree on two of the entries. One of the awards for scholarship at the academy has been divided between two young contestants. Miss Elizabeth Kent. . . ."

"Yes, I know," interrupted dad quickly. "I was the one that voted for the girl. I think she had promise."

"And Miss Elizabeth Kent," announced Nancy placidly, with more truth than grammar, "is *me!*"

CHAPTER II

# Not Enough Cooks

THE girl at the next easel was squeezing paint in big reckless gobs onto an almost brand new palette. Nancy, glancing across, sucked in an envious breath. Cerulean blue at a dollar and a half a tube, Harrison red at a dollar, cobalt . . . the real stuff too, vert green, and a creamy puff of white that she wouldn't use up in a week, much less on a Saturday morning sketch that was a lot smaller than the side of a barn. Nancy groaned inwardly. Oh what a honey of a paint box, big and roomy with how many? . . . ten, twelve new brushes of the finest grade, a new palette knife, darling little oil cups, the box itself of polished wood like a ripe chestnut. Could it be mahogany? Why, there wasn't a box as fine as that in the entire Art Academy!

Nancy averted covetous eyes, ran a hand already smudged with charcoal through her curly brown hair, tightened the thumb tacks that held sketch paper to drawing board, and having so prepared for action, turned to a long inspection of the model. Then began to swing in, with long sweeps of her fat black charcoal the figure of the Italian woman in a bright plaid shawl. These once-a-week sketch classes were great fun and the only chance for a little "pink antique" of the first year art class to draw from human figures. It was a relief after the dusty antique casts all week.

Half an hour of intense concentration. "Rest!" said the class monitor. Model and class relaxed with a sigh, rose to stretch. Nancy shoved back her chair to get a new angle on her drawing and so couldn't help seeing the sketch that stood on the next easel.

Oh dear, oh dear! Not an ounce of talent, not even the vaguest idea, even after two weeks since the Academy opened, of how to go about starting a sketch. Not even any idea of how to set her palette, for the board was smeared already as though a pussy cat had chased a mouse across it, and the painting . . . as though that had been where the cat had captured its prey. Nancy turned to look at the artist herself. Her name? Oh yes, Susannah Benson, also a pink antique. Well, this Susannah Benson was just wasting her time in an art school.

It was at the end of the next rest period when Boris and Pat came along. "We're the press gang for Stunt Day," they informed Nancy. "We're out for volunteers for the entertainments. But volunteer or not, all first year students have to do something, even if its only Kitchen Police."

Stunt Day combined a kind of mild hazing by the older students with a big spread, given by the first year classes. Everyone contributed a quarter for eats, and local talent was obligatory. "Them as don't volunteer for special service will have their names drawn from a hat," said Boris, ominously jotting down names and special talents on a long slip of paper.

Nancy thoughtfully scratched her ear with the handle of her paint brush and admitted that she could sing a few songs, either in French or Italian, with the guitar which she had acquired one summer when in Italy with her mother. And for the rest, if they needed an extra hand to set tables, fold paper napkins, slice sandwiches or wash lettuce . . . she spread ten fingers starfish fashion, for inspection.

"Thanks." Pat seemed really grateful for the

suggestion, and turned to the next victi
sannah.

"Oh . . . oh I don't do anything, I'm afraid." The girl's very fair skin turned the embarrassed color of a spring radish. "Just . . . just put me down for something in the kitchen."

The press gang had turned its collective back when she murmured, half to the listening Nancy. "But I could cook, I suppose."

Nancy's mouth dropped open. "*Cook!* My stars, why'n't you say so! Hey . . . !" She raised her voice Patwards. Pat turned back. "Hey, believe it or not, here's a damsel admits she can *cook.* You know, combine ingredients such as flour, salt, pepper, milk, and eggs into flavorsome comestables."

"Are you good?" Pat sounded dubious. Good cooks are scarce among art students.

"Yes. Yes. I'm good." Susannah admitted it with such modesty that one couldn't doubt.

The third Saturday of the month was the day set for the party; lunch to be served in the new cafeteria in the Academy basement, stunts afterwards in the long, bleak, cement floored store rooms where endless ranks of half finished canvases lined the walls on either side. There was some sort of affair in the upstairs auditorium that afternoon, Pat told Nancy, or they'd have preferred it as more convenient, but chairs could be brought from the cafeteria and she had begged Miss Murdock, in the front office, for the loan of the upstairs piano. Mike, the janitor, could bring that down for them. Quite early in the week Nancy, who rather fancied herself as an organizer, offered her services to Susannah. It was quite a job to feed over a hundred hungry students, the girl would certainly need all the help and advice she could get.

Susannah, smiling a little, murmured "Thank you" in a shy, noncommittal voice and continued to slosh paint on the canvas before her in a way that Nancy would not view without a shudder.

But even though this Benson girl claimed she could cook, she'd be sure to need help in organization. Nancy, unselfishly, valiantly, stood ready to lend her aid whenever a worried Susannah should find that such was needed. Then one morning Susannah produced her list of necessities. So many pounds of potato chips, so many pounds of biscuit flour, of cake flour, so many cans of tomato juice cocktails figured on so many ounces per portion. So many loaves of bread, so many heads of lettuce, with the wholesale price of each lot and which wholesale houses would furnish them at the very best price. Nancy, gasping was left high and dry. Already she had heard from one of the illustrators what a task the Stunt Day spread always was, and what a mess the younger students, with no organization and a great deal of terror, made of it.

"Do you think," asked Susannah mildly, "we might submit this to the committee?"

"My goodness, I should think you could," cried Nancy, and forthwith swept the list and Susan down to the basement, told her to wait there, scrambled together a hasty meeting and advised the inexperienced and bewildered first-year students to vote this heaven sent Miss Benson in charge of the entire refreshments. Only too delighted, the group passed the vote unanimously.

Of course after that Nancy needn't have worried. But she did. Early on Saturday morning, garbed in a huge blue and white checked apron, it made you feel more domestic than a smock, and with sleeves rolled up, she appeared in the basement kitchen. But so, it seemed, had Susannah. Perhaps her apron had meeker checks, perhaps her sleeves were rolled less high, but already an array of groceries waited on the long, zinc covered table, already lettuce drained in the sink, a huge bowl of some sort of dough was churning in the electric mixer.

"What's—what's that?" asked Nancy.

"I had planned hot biscuits," Susannah explained, switching off the motor.

Biscuits for a hundred and eighty famished artists? Nancy blinked. "And what else," she demanded, fascinated.

"I'm going to make some orange cakes, with icing and I put the ice cream in the freezer last night. See how it tastes, will you? That's a darling." One had scarcely, before this, heard Susannah speak above a whisper.

Thereafter, having sampled the ice cream and found it fit for the gods, Nancy stood by to lend a hand. But no advice, no suggestions were required. Just hands. Once, in the lull of a busy but quite unworried morning she asked, "Where in the world did you learn all this, Susannah?"

"Oh Father runs the chain of Silver Grill Restaurants," admitted Susannah, placidly frosting her seventh cake. "I've always hung round one of the kitchens to try out new dishes. I'd have liked to go to Columbia or somewhere and take a course in Hotel Management, but Mother wants me to be an artist. She says this cooking belongs only to my father's side of the family."

"Oh! Too bad," murmured Nancy sympathetically. Susannah applied frosting to a cake the way she mixed paint on that mahogany palette. Well, it was a good technique, but it didn't work as well when you mixed your colors.

Replete with good food, lavish in their praise of pink antique cookery, the older students dragged their chairs out to the big, barn-like cellar. Long racks of ancient canvases lined the walls, and two eighty watt globes, rigged with dark shades and extension cords extemporized stage spot lights at one end of the room.

Nancy had drawn a place near the beginning of the program, and, once her songs were over, was free to enjoy the rest. She stayed in the wings to help adjust makeup, costumes and wigs. Fun, this was. It was also a grand chance to discover new talent among the younger students, ability to be drawn on for the spring Academy Ball. There were songs and dances, some amateurish, even dull, some really excellent, for though art students may be short on culinary skill, they are unusually observant, excellent mimics, and strong on entertainment. Of course there were the inevitable imitations; Shirley Temple, through Mary Boland and Zasu Pitts to Gable and Montgomery, but swinging off into a clever, biting impersonation of Mr. Henry, who, with his little white goatee and plump vague gestures, taught the Illustration class, of

Gardener of the bangs and brusque heartiness, critic of life class and antiques, and Miss Murdock, all spectacles and mild stammer in the front office. And since only students were present, no feelings were ruffled as the cellar echoed with shouts of appreciation.

Then entered the trick Zebra. "Ladi—eeze and Gen-tle-meen! Posi-tive-ly the On-lee Trick Zee-bra in Cap-tiv-ety!" His wide black and white stripes were as suspiciously regular as those on a summer awning, and his hind legs, which belonged in private life to tall George Gorman, bore little relation to his front legs, suspiciously similar to the plump calves of Boris Jones. But he seemed remarkably trained, sure proof, affirmed his master, of the well recognized intelligence of his species; could leap through hoops, pick out the Queen of Hearts from a spread pack of cards, and, thoroughly remarkable, count by fives to a hundred!

Nancy, hovering in the wings, that is behind the cafeteria door, joined in the crash of applause. The zebra, disintegrating, trotted off stage, followed by his whip-cracking trainer. Nancy peeked through the crack in the door. Yes, there was Cynthia Wanstead nodding back over her shoulder at Chick Dalton, monitor of the Illustration class. Surely that meant there would be an intelligent zebra with heterogeneous legs on the Spring Ball program.

Oh, here was the last act of the afternoon, Helen Jennings and Letty Parsons in black face, wide mobile mouths, black yarn wigs and tattered overalls. As Helen went by she shoved into Nancy's hand the further end of a heavy rope and the animal attached thereto.

"Don't forget the cue," she hissed, and sauntered out onto the stage. Perhaps only Nancy noticed how her knees were quivering.

There followed the usual black-face patter

between two old friends who, not having met for years and years must needs boast of their transcendent success in the world of business. Said Pete, who was Letty, scratching a wooley poll; "Well, you see, Jonah, *my* business is dog food. I make food for dogs. Such good food for dogs, such ree-markable food for dogs that when I fed my own dog on this here dog food of mine, he grew so big that his head reached right up into the White House and his tail wagged way off down there in Florida. Well, you know one day that dog of mine bit the President's daughter and they got skeered and had to shoot him. Boy, I guess it took pretty near the biggest gun in the whole United States Army to shoot that dog o'mine. But they done shoot him. They shoot his head right off. . . ."

Pete paused for emphasis. But before his friend could interrupt, continued impressively. "They shoot him *dead*. And you know what happened? Why I had to send a spatchogram to that dog's tail way off down in Florida to tell it the dog was dead and it could stop waggin'!"

A shout of laughter. Jonah, sadly wagging his head, waited for silence, took up the bragging. "Oh boy, I ain't agoin' to tell you no story about what has happened in the past. No sir, Boy. Am I goin' to tell you about what happened right now and right here! You know I went to India? Well I did. I went to India for to get a tiger. This tiger was so big, and so fierce that every time a hunter went out for to shoot this tiger, the tiger would eat the hunter and all his gun-men and all the elephants what had carried them to the jungle.

"But when I went out to hunt him I just took my penny whistle along." Jonah drew, lingeringly from a capacious pocket a small, red painted whistle and tootled a tentative note on it. "Boy, I played so sweet on that whistle that this tiger came out of that jungle and began to purr and rub round my legs. He purred and he purred—" Jonah unlooped an end of rope from around his arm. "And I tied it round his neck and brought that tame tiger right back home with me. He's so tame now, that tiger, he's just like a kitten, he's so tame."

While Pete, watching, fascinated, trembled with fright, Jonah was pulling on the rope. Back in the 'wings', behind Nancy, it uncoiled and uncoiled, yards and yards and yards of it. Nancy, holding the piece that led to the further end, and the animal beneath her arm, watched and chuckled.

Jonah pulled on the last of the rope. Forth from the wings, tied by a slim string to the further end of the cable marched . . . a tiny, mewing, four weeks-old kitten. But Pete had already fainted from fright.

Well, the Stunt Day spread had made school

history. Thereafter, Nancy heard one of the older, and always somewhat upstage sculptors remark, "other spreads would date from 'the one Susannah Benson cooked for us.' " Other stunt Days would arrive and depart, but never, declared the school, would there be another such feast.

Meanwhile Susannah continued to mix her paints into mud pies, to upset her water-color wash on a newly finished drawing, to break endless sticks of expensive vine charcoal, to rub through her paper with an over-energetic eraser. Impossible to imagine a hand so light and deft with pastry would be so heavy with pencil or brush.

Toward the end of that month occurred the Pembroke episode. Among the scholarships awarded each year in the Academy were two given to the best students in the sculptor class, allowing them to travel a summer in Paris, Germany, England and Italy. For nearly twenty years this scholarship fund had been part of school life, but now there seemed to be some doubt as to its renewal. Old Mr. Pembroke was dead, his son had little interest in artists, certainly none at all in women artists, and though it was reported that he would pay a visit to the school and look over the classes, nobody seemed to have much hope that he would continue to supply funds for the scholarship.

In art school news travels as they say it does among the primitive tribes of Africa or Australia. To the humble ears of a little pink antique came the rumor that Mr. Reginald Pembroke and the Board of Trustees would be guests of the Academy at lunch on the following Wednesday.

Exciting, since it concerned the school. But whether the Pembroke scholarship was renewed or not seemed a concern so remote from the life of a first year student as scarcely to merit comment. Not until the day before the luncheon did it seem to matter, and then only because an order had been posted that the students would please bring their own lunches, that for once the rule against eating sandwiches in the studios would be waived. Picnic lunches; that sounded fun.

"Anyway, Mother's chocolate cake and honey buns will be better than this meat pie," remarked Letty, grimacing over her plate. "Don't know what has got into our Mrs. Kennedy; she generally isn't as heavy on the pastry as all this."

"Mrs. Kennedy's home, sick with tonsilitis," came word from the sculptor's table.

"Tonsilitis!" cried Nancy. But then who'll get the lunch for the trustees tomorrow. And the Pembroke!

Consternation. Exclamations. A stunned silence. But what'll they *do* ". . . meaning; what would Miss Murdock and the front office do"... went from table to table. Nancy grinned to herself and slid from her seat. She had had an idea, positively an inspiration. If only it could be pulled off. . . .

Capturing a puzzled Susannah, tucking one hand firmly beneath a reluctant elbow, Nancy dragged her down the hall to face Miss Murdock. "Look here," she began without preamble, and without even pausing to break the news to her victim. "Who's going to get the lunch for the Trustees tomorrow?"

Miss Murdock threw up her hands in despair. She'd been trying all morning to get the Board Committee to agree that they move the lunch party over to the Stratford. Two of the Committee were willing, but one of them, Mrs. Benson, thought it a needless expense. . . .

"Mother!" Susannah was heard to murmur. "I'd forgotten she was on the Board."

"She says," continued Miss Murdock. "Just

to give them 'what the children themselves have every day!' "

"Well, you can't do that if you want to land the Pembroke," agreed Nancy practically. "Report hath it that he's fond of his food. Susannah did a grand job, a historic job with the Stunt Day spread. Why not let her take charge tomorrow. . . ."

"Oh!" . . . incredible, relieved agreement from Miss Murdock.

"Oh!" incredulous, immediate dismay from Susannah.

Nancy nodded firmly to the office head. "You leave it to us," she said. "Just furnish the figures and the funds and we'll bring home the bacon. Eh, Susannah?" and still with a firm hand she bobbed Susannah's head, once, in a nod of agreement.

Susannah grinned, reluctantly. "We . . . ll, it would be kind of fun," she agreed. "But, oh heavens, don't you ever let Mother know!"

"Not a breath of the scandal shall tarnish your fair name," swore Nancy solemnly, and dragged her off to the empty echoing basement for consultation.

Hasty organization assembled a group of helpers from the first year class, Pat, Letty, Ernestine and Nancy herself, in bright new smocks would serve the luncheon. Rapidly, with the skill of a good painter setting her palette Susannah checked the cafeteria's dishes, made long lists of required articles, as tested on paper, discarded and rewrote her menu. A grilled platter; English mutton chops, thick and juicy, little sausages, a slice of tender pink ham, a strip of bacon, a round of grilled pineapple. Then candied carrots, asparagus . . . out of season but you could get it in the frosted foods, big baked potatoes with a lump of lucious butter melting in the creamy heart of each. This, she affirmed was to be a man's luncheon, not a collection of tea room tidbits. No dessert, just the best coffee one could make, hot and lots of it, and a big cheese board with three kinds of crackers and a half dozen varieties of odd cheeses.

Early Wednesday morning Nancy found her, already engulfed in preparations and vast apron, rubbing garlic in the salad bowl, the groceries piled up beside her on the long table, lettuce and salad greens draining in a clean white towel.

"Dash! They've only sent four cheeses," Letty, excused from classes for the occasion was checking the groceries as she unpacked. "And what'll we use for a cheese board, Susan?"

"Go up and see if you can get a clean new little drawing board from the supply shop, Nancy." Susannah scarcely glanced up from her labors.

"Only two packages of asparagus," reported Letty. "Note here says that's all they have in stock, large quantities should be ordered ahead."

"Go out and get a good quantity of broccoli, Pat, will you please?" Susannah poured in olive oil with a lavish hand. "I'll whip up a hollandaise sauce. . . ."

Heavens, how that morning flew! Tables were shoved together to make one banquet board; chairs counted, put into place; silver, shining new polished by Letty, set out, plates and paper napkins made ready. Miss Murdock sent down two giant bunches of tawny chrysanthemums which must be arranged. And as the feminine voices of the Trustees mingled with the firm tones of Mr. Pembroke and the few masculine members sounded in the upper corridors, were heard descending the stairs, the four waitresses slipped into smocks of tan and brown, yellow and orange, powdered shiny noses and crowded behind the kitchen door to await their cues.

"What's he like?" Susannah, tasting spoon in

hand, leaned past Nancy to peer through the crack in the door.

"Plumpish, roll at the back of his neck, not in the least dyspeptic," reported Nancy in a hopeful whisper. "Oh, look at his partner will you? There's a lady who knows her own mind. See, the one in the mink collar," and then could have bitten off her tongue as Susannah murmured apologetically. "That's mother. Yes, she does get her own way! Now go on in, my hearties, and don't spill the salad on Mr. Pembroke's grey trousers. Remember, the fate of four painters and sculptors hangs on this luncheon."

For the next hour Nancy, whose post was at the head of the table, was too busy to do more than report in brief trips to the kitchen. "Your biscuits are voted a masterpiece, Susan. . . . One of the trustees has eaten the salad on both sides of his plate. Have we got any more out here? . . .

More broccoli, and lots of the sauce for Mr. Pembroke. . . . The lady in the lavandar tweed wants to know where we got our English mutton chops? . . . Any more biscuits, Susan? . . . Oh bless you," as they came, hot and smoking from the oven. And again. "Mr. Pembroke wants some more of the broccoli please. And just two more biscuits. Heavens, the man will ruin his supper!"

In between she must keep her ears open for gossip of the scholarship. There was plenty of talk about it, but no decision seemed to have been made, and whenever the conversation seemed liable to wander to other subjects Mrs. Benson gave skillful chase, pounced on it, brought it triumphantly back.

"So pretty, the girls in their fresh little smocks," she murmured sentimentally. "Don't you think so, Mr. Pembroke? My own little daughter is too busy of course to be among them.

So hard working . . . she belongs to a class with such a quaint name . . . you'll be amused at this I'm sure. They call themselves the 'pink antiques' . . . one of the higher classes of course. Great talent . . . in another year she may be in line for your splendid scholarship. . . ."

Nancy, choking back her laughter, escaped to the kitchen.

At last it was over, the final coffee cup set down, the final cigarette extinguished in saucer, hands clutched at handbags, wraps were retrieved from the backs of chairs, chair legs scraped on the tiled floor, the last trustee, with many false starts and haltings, disappeared through the door. Mr. Pembroke's high laugh echoed back from the hall.

Nancy sank into the nearest chair, Pat flopped on a window sill, Ernestine and Letty trooped in from the kitchen.

"Well, it went off all right," began Nancy.

"Went off all right? It went like a breeze, like a hurricane!" Pat came to life for a moment. "The dear man managed six biscuits and gazed longingly at the empty plate. But I felt that even one more would be dangerous, with that waistline."

"He had two helpings of the asparagus," Letty remembered. "I could manage with two or three stalks myself. Oh, here's our Susannah. What on earth . . .?"

For Susannah's arms strained with a crowded tray; a hot grill for each of them, piping hot biscuits, a big potato apiece, asparagus with hollandaise sauce since the two packages would do for five of them. And besides that a big pitcher of milk and a huge chocolate cake that had somehow got itself baked, cooled and frosted.

"This is for us," she said, sliding it onto the cluttered table. Nancy, reviving miraculously, leaped to remove the soiled dishes.

"Susannah, you'll have wings, you'll positively have wings," breathed the famished Pat as Ernestine and Letty joined with yelps of appreciation. Thereafter comparative silence as five little pink antiques sought to emulate Mr. Pembroke's biscuit record. Then Pat's curiosity began to consume her.

"I'd give a five pound tube of zinc white, Winsor and Newton preferred, to know what they're saying about the scholarships upstairs," she declared, returning her plate for more cake.

"Surely they won't decide anything today." Nancy poured herself another glass of milk.

"Yes they will. The Academy has to know almost immediately." That was the reason, said Ernestine, why the luncheon couldn't be postponed. "Susan, you certainly did us proud. Why on earth you should want to be a half-baked artist when you're already a full fledged cook is something I can't imagine!"

"I don't," Susannah's mild little voice was unexpectedly firm. "It's just an idea of Mother's. For myself, I hate every minute of it. But you can't convince her that cooking is also an art."

Poor kid, thought Nancy. Not to be able to work at what she wanted most.

"Look here," Pat was taking off her smock. "I'm going to slip upstairs to listen at doors and hang about the fringes," and was gone.

Nancy, half asleep with the pleasant relaxation that comes from a full meal after fatigue, helped herself to crackers and cheese and decided against trying to work on her cast drawing before she went home. Today had held excitement enough. Letty, gathering up plates and saucers was blessing Mike's sister, who had volunteered to do the dishes. Then Pat's head, like a cuckoo out of a clock popped through the doorway. "Henry and Pembroke and two trustees are in a huddle outside illustration class," she squeaked breathlessly. "I heard 'scholarships' mentioned. Didn't dare hover any nearer. He's visited all the classes," she popped off again.

Almost immediately she reappeared. "Susannah, he wants *you*." she cried.

"Me? . . . Why? . . . What for?" stammered Susannah.

"He wants your recipe for hollandaise sauce."

Susannah turned helplessly to Nancy. "Oh Nancy, Mother's there. She'll find out what I've been doing. Nancy, I can't ever in the world . . . " she began.

"This is Die for Dear Old Rutgers I guess. You've got to, Susan. Why, it might mean all the difference between our getting the scholarships, and not."

Susannah nodded miserably, seemed to set her jaw firmly, and taking off her apron plodded blindly ahead, up the stairs. Straight to the group by the class room door. She halted. "Mr. Pembroke," she began, feebly, almost in a whisper. Then started once more, this time more loudly. "Mr. Pembroke."

Mrs. Benson's face was beaming. "My little girl, Mr. Pembroke. You remember, I told you . . ." she was beginning when suddenly Susannah, recovering her voice, interrupted firmly. "I'm the cook." Her voice was a flat statement. "You wanted a recipe?"

The great man was pompously congratulatory. "My felicitations, young woman," he began as one who faces a battery of microphones. "Felicitations on embarking in a profession that is really the Crown, the Glory of Womanhood." He put it all into capitals, like that. "The world will never have sufficient of good cooks. Now that sauce hollandaise," descending from the platform to the more personal touch, "can you tell me. . . ." He seemed to savor it again between his full red lips.

Nancy's gaze, fascinated, fastened on the face of Mrs. Benson. Such variety of emotions were flitting across that not unpleasantly open countenance. Pride, at her daughter's appearance. Chagrin and dismay that the rôle had proved so humble, so little of the artiste. Then the beginning of something, was it pride? again.

"That's easy," said Susannah plainly. "You tell your cook she probably doesn't beat it enough. The trick is just to keep on beating it, in the double boiler, every time she adds another egg yolk. It must be smooth you know, like a well made custard."

Mr. Pembroke's pencil was out, he scribbled, muttering the directions as they came to him. Nancy, glancing again at Mrs. Benson's face felt that now it might be safe to withdraw. Perhaps now things might be a little better for Susannah.

Feeling that today could hold little more, limp from so much excitement, she slipped along the mattinged hallway and dodging the half dozen sculptors who lingered, curious, in their doorway, slid into the cloakroom to hang up her smock and smooth her hair. Behind her the door flapped open again. It was Susannah. But what a Susannah!

Radiant, with shining eyes, seemingly a full inch taller. "Listen, Nancy, it's going to be all right. I don't have to fool with this nonsense any longer. She says so. Mother says so. I'm to start on Hotel Management as soon as we can get my papers made out. The exams will be easy, I won't have any trouble with them." Confident, of a sudden, was Susannah.

"Well! Well! I mean . . ." Nancy gulped, blinking. "Good for you, Susy. This was all pretty sudden, wasn't it?"

"Mr. Pembroke decided it I guess. He says

he'll renew the scholarships all right, because there must be quite a few people in the world who wouldn't ever be good cooks and they might as well go to art school and learn to do something else, even if it isn't so useful." She seemed quite serious about all this, was reaching down her hat and cloak, beside her on the floor the big mahogany paint box. She turned, to speak over her shoulder. "You've been just a peach about all this, Nancy Brewster. I'll never forget it. I hope you go on and make a success of this drawing and painting. If that's what you want," she added generously. "Look here, can you use this thing do you think?" Anxiously she thrust the wide leather handle of the box into Nancy's unresisting hand. "Because I never shall want to open it again. Now I've got to run and catch up with Mother. Nothing like," she added with bright originality, "striking while the iron is hot!" And dashed off.

Nancy, leaning limply against the wall was still recovering her breath and about to make up her mind to examine her new found treasure when the door flapped open again. Perhaps . . . but no, it was only Letty.

"What's that you've got there, Nancy?" she asked curiously. "You look as though someone had left you a legacy."

"Someone has," said Nancy, kneeling down to slide open the little brass hooks of the treasure chest. "Now just you watch me break into illustration class. What's a handicap for a cook may be sheer inspiration for a painter!"

## CHAPTER III

# *A Wig for Montezuma*

NANCY sighed and shifted her weight to the other foot. The change wasn't much help; the left ached as much as the right. She shifted back again.

"If I'd been old Montezuma I'd have hung the palace with green cheesecloth and called it a day," she grumbled good naturedly and sloshed another long streak of blue, water color paint on the palace pillars.

Clarabel Adams smiled wearily, and pushing back the lock of pale hair that always dropped forward again, over her eyes, made another smudge across her nose. "I'm tired too. There isn't much in this Pink Antique business, is there? All work and no play, if you ask me!"

"It's all for the honor of the Art Academy, my children, and next year you also shall reap the reward." Chick was head of the Pageant committee and chief performer, but he shouldn't, thought Nancy, sneak up like that on a fellow. 'Twasn't fair. Why we might have been talking about him!

"Gracious," she murmured as he passed on down the big Hall. "I didn't know we were overheard. But I do think it's a shame the lower classes . . . like us . . . did you know we were members of the lower classes, honey? . . . have to labor like slaves for their party, and then not even get a dab of pink ice cream!"

But Clarabel Adams was less rebellious. From the perilous peak of her stepladder she gazed sentimentally after the departing Chick, with what Nancy privately considered a "dying calf" expression. "Isn't he wonderful?" she murmured to the scoffing Nancy. "And how that boy can paint!" then returning to things mundane, "Nan, give me some more of that color will you? I've been scraping the bottom of this pail for the past five minutes."

"Then it's high time we walked out," declared the more independent Nancy. "I'm hungry as a clothes moth. Coming, Harold?" to her neighbor on the other side. "Oh, come along. Three little Pink Antiques won't be missed by that old Simon Legree."

In the big Academy Hall matters were in train for the Thanksgiving dance and pageant, given and attended by all the upper classes of the Art Academy. Sculptors, painters, illustrators and members of the life class might buy tickets, if they could afford them, or if, on the other hand, they had talents such as dancing or singing that might add glory and honor to the performance, they could get in free. But the Pink Antiques, mere first-year students who spent their daylight hours drawing from the great, dusty gray antique casts that stood like oversized ghosts along the walls of the First Year class room, were barred. They might work, in fact they had all been drafted for service slapping paint on the paper-muslin hangings that were to change the Hall into a Court of Ancient Mexico, but they were considered too young and unimportant to attend the ball itself. Most of them didn't mind, deeming it sufficient honor to be asked to labor alongside such real artists as Chick Dalton and such illustrators as Cynthia Wanstead. But Nancy was made of more rebellious stuff. Besides she had known artists and painters all her life and hadn't a grain of proper awe and respect for any of 'em.

Back in the girls' dressing room Nancy slipped out of her paint daubed smock and into a dark blue silk trimmed with tricky little edgings and frillings of red, ran a comb through her fluffy brown bob, powdered her nose, washed her hands and even had her hat in her hand before Clarabel had shed her charcoal tinged apron.

"Goodness, child! Do hurry, Harold will be starving on the mat."

"You go ahead and keep him amused," suggested the slower Clarabel, who always got nervous when she was hustled. "I'll hurry all I can. Honest."

Nancy slid her arms into the armholes of her winter coat and hunched it over her shoulders. "Okay . . . but do hustle," and let the door flap behind her. Her feet were silent on the dingy cocoa matting that carpeted the cement hallway and as she passed the modeling room, first on the right, she heard no sound of voices, no slap of wet palms on damp clay. Almost every class room was empty, almost every class busy in the big Hall, rushing the decorations that they might be done in time for the party, two days off. She saw Chick Dalton's tousled head emerge from the door of the stage entrance to the Hall, saw him glance up and down the passage and thought that here was a good chance to tackle him alone. Perhaps something could be managed . . . two tickets, just two, ple-ease kind mister . . .

But someone else had cornered him first. Gussy Edwards must have been watching for him from the open door of the painters' class, across the hall. She was one of the older students, a big boned, high shouldered German girl, who rather fancied herself as a future motion picture star, and had been aptly cast for a leading part in the pageant.

Nancy, hanging back, waited. She'd like to get Chick alone if she could, and Gussy probably only wanted to ask some question about the show—no very pleasant one, by her expression.

But Gussy had a real grievance. Her arrogant voice echoed clearly down the empty corridor.

"And you needn't think, Chick Dalton, that you can add to your part, by taking away some of mine . . . "

Chick's back was now toward Nancy but she could see him shrug his shoulders. "Nothing of the sort," his voice was low, less penetrating than the irate Gussy's. "It was just that the committee felt the whole show was too long . . . you were there, so you ought to know it was by popular vote. Someone's part had to be cut; if we start at midnight, and expect to be through before morning, and you're not the only one who lost a few lines."

"You cut two songs, and three pages of speech from mine . . . and only one song from yours!"

"Oh, for the love of Pete. I can't stay here and argue. Got to get back to rehearsal." Chick abruptly turned and walked away. It was the wisest thing he could do, admitted Nancy. Gussy was just spoiling for a scene. But Gussy had slammed back into the painters' room and an angry sob floated back over her shoulder.

As Nancy caught up with Chick he remarked, "She needn't think she can act like a tragedy queen!" His tone was slightly apologetic as Nancy couldn't have helped overhearing. "Going to lunch, young one? Well, don't take too long. We need every hand on deck."

"Slave driver!" Nancy made a little face. "Look here, Mr. Dalton . . . " one was always respectful, at least to their faces, to upper classmen. "How about two tickets for the dance? I can pay for them."

"No sir! Not to Antiques. Sorry, but those are the rules. Only older students and the Fellowship alumni."

"Fellowship? Oh . . . well." Nancy abruptly

switched the subject. "Look here, you better watch out for Gussy Edwards. She's got an awful temper and she may make trouble."

Chick seemed unworried. "Nonsense, I can handle that. Just a bit of temperament. Don't you ruffle your curls about her. Hello, Harold! How's the boy?" and passed on down the corridor.

From beyond the wall came a sudden roar and stamp as the chorus broke into rehearsal of their welcome to their King. "Monty . . . Monty . . . Monty . . . zum . . . aaa!" It was a good song . . . and a perfectly swell dance. Nancy grabbed Harold and spun him the length of the corridor in a galloping fox trot, then back again, heavy winter coat, hat, gloves and all.

"Why," she cried suddenly stopping dead. "Why, Harold, you're a perfectly scrumptious dancer!"

"Sure, why not?" Harold always got very

red and very gruff, more booming-voiced than usual, when he was embarrassed. "I can dance . . . why not, I love it."

"Oh, I don't know. Oh, here comes Cold Molasses," which, because of its slowness, was of course Clarabel. The name was not Nancy's invention, it had just, somehow, grown of itself. But Harold's nickname of the Third Conspirator, out of any Shakespeare tragedy, had been her own idea. With that deep booming voice of his Harold would have made such a ridiculous conspirator; why if he just whispered in the long corridor every one in all four classes heard what the secret was about.

Which was why, next day, when Nancy wanted to do a little conspiring of her own, she dragged Harold out to lunch with her again. "This is Dutch, of course," she stated the invariable rule of Academy lunches. "And if you're hard up, we can go to the Automat, but

I'd like the Pewter Pitcher and to get away from everybody. I want to talk to you."

"The Pitcher is all right," growled Harold good naturedly. "But why all the mystery?"

Nancy giggled and gave a pleased little skip, right there on Fortnum street. "You wait, I'll show you," and once lunch had been decided upon, and the waitress had departed with an order for two club sandwiches, a chocolate sundae with marshmallow cream and walnuts, and one hot fudge surprise . . . Nancy leaned across the table. With the air of one conspirator to another she opened her purse and took out an envelope. Opened the envelope and took out two familiar dark green tickets.

She glanced hastily over one shoulder, then over the other and, to be quite sure, lifted the cloth and peered beneath the table. Then under the shelter of her napkin, passed the two tickets across to the puzzled Harold, who took them.

He regarded them a moment, frowning in incredulous amazement. "Gee whillikins, Nan, where'd you get these? Why, they're for the Montezuma Ball!"

"Oh . . . " Nancy's mouth was demure, her eyes dancing. "That's a secret. Will you go with me, kind sir?"

"Sure will. You're a peach of a dancer," he conceded not ungallantly. "But . . . "

"We'll have to," Nancy spoke in a tense stage whisper though no Academy student was within distance of a small shout, "go in disguise. No one must know we're Pink Antiques." Her hand went out to recover the tickets.

"Sure," assented Harold, the matter of fact. "That's all right. We've got to wear costumes anyway, haven't we?"

Nancy leaned back and nodded. "I'll help with that. Mother,—oh well, I might as well tell you, the tickets are Mother's. She . . . she belongs to the Academy Fellowship. She graduated from there you know."

"Oh, does she?" Harold was properly impressed. Nancy with her usual love of mystery had, so far, kept her famous mother concealed from the other students. "Mother says she doesn't mind as long as we keep it quiet. She thinks that the Pink Antiques ought to be allowed to go anyway, but as long as she had tickets, and couldn't go, why then I thought I might as well use them. Now as to costume," she continued. "You'll have to shave off that moustache, Harold."

Harold's hand went caressingly to the adornment of his upper lip, to the pride of his life. "Oh but . . . "

"It's got to go," stated Nancy flatly. "No Montezuman or Aztecian wore a moustache. Bumpy Powers is cutting off his for the evening and his is bigger than yours. Besides," she offered plentiful consolation, "it'll come in stronger and longer than ever. And then your eyebrows . . . well, not shave 'em, but take some of them off . . . "

Harold's brows were blond, but bristling. No grease paint could cover them. They'd be, simply, a complete giveaway to the sharp and discerning eyes of his fellow students. "Oh, all right," agreed Harold. "But this has got to be some dance, to make up."

"It's going to," promised Nancy brightly and rashly. "Now for the rest of the costume . . . " and with further delighted air of secrecy, turned to the next important problem.

It was rather a rush to get ready. Nancy had to stay away from school the final day to complete her costume, and as the Brewsters lived out of town, she accepted Clarabel's invitation to spend the night with her.

"I'll speak to my landlady about it, and she

can give you a key, so you can come in as late as you like," promised the hostess. "Hope you won't mind sharing the bed with me, it's a nice wide one."

"Just so there's lots of hot water after midnight," and at the other's look of bewilderment, "I'll be wearing a luscious brown makeup and if it won't come off with cold cream and hot water before I turn in, your landlady'll think you've been eating chocolate cake in bed."

Clarabel giggled. "I'll ask Mrs. O'Neill about that. She's a dear old thing and doesn't mind what you do. But where is Harold going to put on his makeup?"

"You'd better speak to Mrs. O'Neill about that too. Ask her if she'd mind if he came to the house, so I can paint his features for the party."

Mrs. O'Neill, plump and rosy as a winter apple, immaculate in starched blue gingham that rustled frostily, bobbed in and out all during Nancy's elaborate preparations. She came ostensibly to see "if the young lady needed anything," but her "For the love of Mary!" "My hivens, think o' that now!" and "My saints, such goin's on as they must have had in thim days!" were so amusing and she was so interested that Nancy began to ask her advice and assistance, that the nice old thing might linger and see the entire preparation.

With her famous mother's help, Nancy had chosen the costume of a possible, and certainly most decorative, Aztec princess. The color scheme of blue and silver was relieved and accented by garlands of bright flowers and little tinkling silver bells which formed bracelets at ankles, below the knees, on bare wrists and upper arms. Nancy slipped these on first, then over her head the knee length costume, painted and splashed in bright colors in imitation of the fabulous Aztec feather work. There was a long and very decorative cloak of rayon, silky and floaty, also colored like birds' feathers, which clasped on the shoulder beneath a great, strangely shaped buckle in imitation jade.

"We don't really know what the Aztec women dressed like," she told the fascinated Mrs. O'Neill. "We can know the warriors' costumes by the pictures of them, in tombs and temples. But they never painted any women. This won't look so silly when I've finished my make-up and got on the wig and headdress."

"Think o' that now," murmured the admiring audience and sat herself on the bed to watch this transformation of a little pink antique into an ancient bit of Mexican royalty.

The make-up seemed very dark in contrast to Nancy's fluffy light brown hair, but when she had slicked back every lock and pinned it into a tight flat mass at the top of her head, moistening her hands to flatten every lock away from her forehead, she pulled on the wig. It was of short, curled yarn strands that clung close to her cheeks. Once adjusted to her satisfaction and with an additional touch of rouge, lipstick and eyebrow pencil, the wig seemed to fit like the final piece slipped into a jigsaw puzzle.

"But wait till you see my crown." Nancy opened a large hatbox and took it out. The waving feathers, some standing high, some trailing down over shoulders and back were predominantly silver-tipped blue, darker than the costume. Heavy pendants of lapis and dull silver hung down like enormous earrings, and around her neck she clasped a flat necklace to match that added the final note of color and dash to the costume.

"Now!" Eyes bright with excitement she stood back and pirouetted, with little dancing steps, to be admired, strutting like a peacock.

"It's simply heavenly, Nan!" Clarabel's tone was almost reverent. "You'll be the Belle of the ball. And not a soul will recognize you. Only—your voice?"

"Oh, I can manage that, if I'm careful." Nancy spoke deeply, from her chest. "It's going to be fun, too. Oh, there's the doorbell. Will you let him up, if it's Harold, Mrs. O'Neill? He'll need some make-up too. Clarabel, kick those shoes and stockings under the bed. You can stay and watch this too, Mrs. O'Neill."

She was smoothing the make-up around her eyes when Harold's conspiratorial tones sounded in the hallway.

"In here?" he asked, and Nancy turned to face him. Then at the sight that met her eyes she clutched the dressing table behind her, choking with suppressed laughter. Suppressed because tears, even of mirth would streak and destroy her carefully made up face, and because, also, she might hurt Harold's feelings. But he didn't seem to mind.

"Gosh, I know I look funny," he boomed. "Hurry up and put some paint on me; I had to pretend a cold and talk through a handkerchief all the time I was paying the taxi driver. Never felt so undressed in all my life."

There was a white, strangely raw look around the upper lip, and Harold sans moustache and eyebrows was scarcely recognizable.

It was in the midst of making new eyebrows, dark and heavy, meeting over the nose and completely transforming his generally mild expression, that Nancy had another thought, a terrible one. "Look here, we're supposed to be in disguise. . . ."

"Gosh, don't I know that?" protested Harold, wincing under the onslaught of her pencil. "You've told me about ten times.

Ouch . . . do you have to rub that in so hard?"

"Sorry. But about the disguise . . . you won't be able to talk, you know." She broke it to him gently.

"My goodness, that's so," agreed Clarabel. "Anybody'd know his voice!"

"For the love of Pete, haven't I made enough sacrifice for this dance?" Harold's tone was plaintive. "D'you expect me to go dumb all the evening?"

"That won't be so hard. No, listen here . . . honest. . . ." Nancy sat down to argue the point. "I can be the Aztec princess and you can be my dumb . . . don't giggle Clara . . . dumb slave or something. . . ."

"Or something is right. Okay, I don't care. Only the dances and the eats have to be extra special good to make up for all this. First my moustache, then my eyebrows and now my voice. What next?" he asked resignedly.

"Next is this lipstick." Nancy returned to the onslaught.

"And did them Aztec men use lipstick too?" queried the bewildered Mrs. O'Neill.

But once it was all over, and the two paused for a moment's regard of their splendor in the long mirror at the foot of the stairs, even Harold was impressed by all their glory. "Don't believe old Montezuma himself will look any better," he approved.

"That's the boy." Nancy squeezed his arm and pulled him toward the door. "Come on. We'll have to leave before the final dance but we can get in a lot before the midnight show goes on."

Their taxi driver, much amused, drew up at last before an unfamiliar awning that transformed the entrance to the Art Academy. Small urchins and older spectators crowded the fringes of the entrance but they wriggled through to the door, and once their tickets had passed the door keeper's eagle-eyed inspection Nancy drew a sigh of relief.

"Well, that's over," she murmured. "Doesn't the place look grand? Hurry and get out of your coat and hat and I'll meet you opposite the illustration class door." She gave him a little shove, then ran after him to whisper into his ear an emphatic "*Don't talk!* Don't say *one word!*" and thought to herself, "That's kind of mean, for him. I'll have to see that he has an extra good time."

The corridors were hung with gray paper muslin marked off like great blocks of stone and making a neutral background that threw out all the bright and gorgeous costumes thronging down them. But no amount of gorgeousness, no amount of silks and satins nor perfume and lipstick and powder could completely disguise the old Academy and its characteristic smell;

turps and wet clay, canvas and oil, charcoal and varnish. Nancy sniffed it with delight.

Gussy Edwards swept by. No one could mistake those high shoulders, that arrogant walk. Her dress was Incan, not Aztec, but would be changed later for the pageant. Though she was laughing with her partner she looked sullen and sulky beneath the present mood and Nancy wondered if she had recovered from her wrath.

There was Cynthia Wanstead, in flame color and brown, and Eve, of the red hair, both members of the illustration class.

They turned with frank stares for Nancy's costume but failed to recognize her beneath it. This was fun, she thought, biting on the inside of her dimple lest it peep out and betray her. This was lots of fun; like wearing an invisible cloak, like being an audience for an unsuspecting play. She was, so far, completely incognito.

"Well, well, what humming bird's nest brought you out?" That was Chick Dalton himself.

"Oh, my Lord Montezuma!" Nancy's curtsey was deep and her chest tones successful.

"And who might you be?" Chick peered under the disguising headdress.

"Foreign royalty," murmured Nancy. "And here comes my dumb slave. Perhaps we shall meet later," and on Harold's proffered arm swept away toward the music and the dance.

"How did you get along?" she asked in the waltz. "I mean without talking?"

"All right," he whispered in such a hoarse shout that Nancy realized Harold must remain altogether silent, even with her. Two couples had whirled to gaze at them even as they danced. "I'm afraid it won't do," she murmured ruefully. "You'll have to let me do all the conversing, don't even whisper!"

The decorations in the big Hall were a great success. Nancy danced with a visiting architect, who told her so, and congratulated her on, what she told him, was her part in it. No need to be secret here. He would never suspect her of being a mere Pink Antique. He demanded if she were going to be in the pageant but Nancy shook her head.

"No, but it'll be the best one they've ever had." Every year's pageant was always that. Then she noted Gussy, lowering like an ornamental thundercloud, as she swept by on the arm of Stephen Kent, the famous author. He failed to recognize Nancy. She began to feel quite safe. If Harold was all right. . . .

But Harold had proved to be quite amenable, in fact was enjoying this as much as Nancy. "It's kind of fun, being dumb," he admitted when for a moment they found a safely isolated corner of the long corridor. "But gosh this wig is hot. How do you stand yours?"

"The wig's all right but every partner I've had has complained that the feathers tickle his ears. Guess I'll remove the crown and just wear the wig now." Originally the height had added to her masquerade but she felt that now she could safely dispense with that. She saw Harold, back on the floor, waltzing with a little blond stranger all in red and purple, refused two offers for her own dance and sped down the corridor.

She would like to leave the headdress in her locker, but was afraid to be discovered before the door of it. Still, if she could whisk it in, and later remove it, wrapped in a bundle like an old canvas—she passed the locker and looked back. The corridor was almost empty save for some men quietly talking and smoking at the further end. Now was the time.

Nancy twirled the combination lock and

opened the door a small crack, ready to clap it shut should someone come along. All was still safe. She opened it wider and crouching down tugged at her headdress. It was tight and yes, it was hot too. She'd be glad to get out of it. But the chinstrap and the long swinging earrings became entangled in the yarn of her wig and for a long moment she struggled, hot and bothered, to free herself.

Approaching footsteps sounded on the cement floor. No voices; that meant just one person, probably. Nancy was free at last and dropping the headdress on the floor of her locker gazed out like a small ostrich, the metal door half concealing her.

The passerby was Gussy Edwards already in her pageant dress. She was alone, but she was quite liable to recognize Nancy's locker, and later on put two and two together. And no one would be more willing to make trouble than

Gussy . . . if she got a chance. Nancy wished the cupboard wasn't so full of junk . . . she'd like to crawl completely inside.

The girl, however, paid no attention to Nancy, in fact she seemed quite as anxious to escape attention. Halfway along the hall was an archway; she paused a moment there to glance back, almost furtively. Nancy waited. Gussy came on, her high heels tap-tapping sharply on the cement floor, for tonight clear of the matting, passed the locker, on toward the dressing room at the end. Nancy slipped from behind the shelter of her door, crashed it shut, twirled the lock into place. Gussy had disappeared.

What time was it? Nearly midnight? From the big Hall sounded the call of a trumpet. That meant the pageant was about to begin. . . . Gussy, as one of the principals, should have been behind the stage ready to go on. Nancy didn't dare to follow her to the dressing room, but scurried to the entrance to the Hall. The dancing had stopped. Straw mats were being distributed to those who wished to sit on the floor and the benches along the three walls were full. Harold had secured a seat near the front and as Nancy caught his eye, crooked a beckoning finger. But she shook her head, made a cryptic gesture that was meant to tell him she'd be back and slipped out again.

The dressing room at the end of the hall was deserted. Gussy had gone. Nancy sniffed around. There probably wasn't a clue in sight, even if, giggled Nancy to herself, there had been a crime. But "I've got a hunch. . . . I've got a hunch," she crooned to herself.

Cloaks of the students lined two walls. The big general dressing room, where Nancy had left her things was in the front office, converted for this evening. What cloak had Gussy worn?

she wondered. Not anything that Nancy could recognize. She moved along the walls, giving each coat a gentle shake, but without result. Well, it was probably none of her business and she'd better hurry back or she'd miss the pageant. She turned to the wide mirrors above the wash basins to repair her make-up, if it needed it. But that was all right too. Over her shoulder she could see the dark coats, velvet and satin and fur, hanging straight and still from their pegs. And below one of them something black and small on the cement floor.

Nancy turned and swooping, picked it up. It was a wig, much like her own, of black yarn on a black net base, now so torn and twisted that it would be quite useless. Where had it come from? Nancy tossed it back on the floor. What had it been doing there . . . and what small dark thing had Gussy held in her hand as she hurried past Nancy's locker? She was puzzled.

With brain working furiously she strolled up toward the Hall. The big door was open for ventilation and she could see that the stage curtain was up. Bright lights, greenish blue, reflected on the faces of the audience. From Nancy's end of the Hall, the end near the stage entrance, were the entrances to the stage dressing rooms, the usual small rooms back of the stage further augmented by screens and curtains to make enough space for the chorus. Nancy, still puzzling, shoved aside a curtain and looked in.

She was not acquainted with the exact progress of the pageant, but from the rehearsals, which had been going on for two weeks, and from odd bits she had overheard here and there, she could piece together something of its sequence. There would be the opening chorus, the one they were singing now, with all the courtiers; then a short conversation between the

Queen, who was Gussy, and the Captain of the Guard. Then another chorus and a dance, and finally the entrance, in full state, of Montezuma himself. That was Chick Dalton, who had cut down, or so Gussy had claimed, the part of the Queen, and who even now, should be all ready for his entrance.

Nancy wondered. She shoved aside the curtain a little further and went in.

Two long planks on trestles took up much of the space. They were piled with a heterogeneous collection of feathered cloaks, headdresses, make-up boxes, odd sandals, fans and other things. Obviously this was the place where the chorus had added the finishing touch to their costumes. No one was here save little Barbara Bennet, who was lame and unable to take part in the stage show, and always did make-up and prompters' parts. Her back was toward Nancy and her whole attention on the stage and on the prompt book in her hands.

Noiseless as a shadow Nancy slipped around the tables, made for the small dressing rooms beyond. The chorus was ended and the boys and girls trooping off the stage, and crowded into the shadow of a wing to watch. Gussy was on stage now, wouldn't come off, if Nancy remembered rightly, until later in the act. Chick must be in his dressing room.

The chorus, crowding in the wings, was silent; Barbara held up a cautioning hand. No whisper from the wings must mar Gussy's speech on the stage. Nancy faced the chorus, who did not see her. The boys wore long cloaks of royal blue, short tunics, wide gilt bands about their hair, and bracelets and sandals of gilt. Each had a wig, similar to the one Nancy had found in the dressing room and each wig was in its proper place. Nancy's puzzled eyes counted them once again. Then Gussy's speech was finished, the Captain of the Guard's "Hist! We are overheard!" and the orchestra broke into another tune. The chorus was on the stage again.

Behind Nancy a door slammed shut. Barbara looked across, frowning, her finger on her lips but the shout of the chorus, in full swing of the first verse, would have drowned the noise for the audience. Chick Dalton, in the King's costume, ready to go on, his enormous feathered crown in his hand, stood in the doorway. He looked around wildly. Every other character was on the stage.

Nancy knew what that meant. Every wig was being worn but Montezuma's. And Nancy knew where Montezuma's wig was lying, torn and useless.

Funny how quickly a chorus finished their song, one they had spent days and days to learn! The first verse was over, the first chorus nearly done. Only one more verse. Perhaps the audience would demand an encore. Nancy slipped to the dressing room door, plucked Chick's sleeve and hauled him inside.

"What on earth!" demanded that astonished young man. "Look here, I'm in a hurry. Something's happened to my wig."

"I know." Nancy forgot to use her chest tones, forgot her betraying dimple. "I know all about that. Gussy stole it. Now sit down and we'll see. . . ."

Without waiting to finish her sentence she shoved him into a chair and began to peel off her own wig. It was a tight haul and pulled painfully at the short hairs at the temples but Nancy tugged valiantly—and at last it came away with a jerk.

"Nancy, you little devil! Didn't you know. . . ."

"I know. Pink Antiques and everything.

But I came on Mother's Fellowship ticket and a jolly good thing for you, too! Now shut up, and sit down. We've got to get you into this somehow."

The wig was not so tight as she had feared. Made to go over her abundant curls it fitted his larger head very nicely and was much the same style, black yarn in close black curls, as the King had worn. A burst of applause from the audience signalled that the second chorus was finished. Now would come "Here comes the King." Chick must be on the stage immediately after that. He rose to go but Nancy shoved him back. "Sit down. They've encored it."

So they had. Now for the crown. That took a few minutes to adjust, for Nancy's fingers were shaking with the excitement. The chorus had finished for the second time, the applause was dying down, Chick was halfway to the door before the last feather of his crown was in place, Nancy doing her best to keep up with him.

For just a moment then he paused. "What will you do? You can't go out there without a wig."

"Never mind me. Run along." She gave him a shove. "I'll manage somehow."

"Here comes the King. Hail. Monte. . Monte. . Mont. . . y. . zu. . maaa!"

His Royal Highness disappeared beyond the curve of the wings.

Nancy pulled a chair towards her with her foot and sat down. Now that it was all over she felt, for a moment, just a little bit teary. She would have liked to see that show, her first at the Art Academy. Still there would be another in the spring, and Nancy had no intention of remaining a Pink Antique until spring.

Now for a paper and pencil, one of the hardest things to find where artists work! But Chick had been making notes on his musical score. Nancy tore out a blank back page and scribbled a note, stuck it into the edge of his make-up mirror. Chick would have to repay her by getting word to Harold, since she'd have to cut the remainder of the dance. His scarf, a wide yellow silk one, lay with his coat and hat on a chair; she could borrow that. She wound it around her betraying curls, closed the door softly behind her and slipping behind the unconscious Barbara found herself once more in the corridor.

No one had seen her and the excuse of a sudden toothache would pass her by anyone who might be at the outer door. As it happened even that was unnecessary.

An hour later, free of make-up, and very sleepy, she slipped into bed beside Clarabel. She hoped she wouldn't waken her.

But Clarabel did rouse, finally, and turn drowsily to ask, "'Lo, Nancy . . . what's the matter? Are you laughing?"

"How long does it take eyebrows to grow?"

"I don't know. A month maybe."

"Poor Harold," murmured Nancy, sleepily.

## CHAPTER IV

# *Penny Wisdom*

"And since it's Henry's twenty-fifth anniversary as head of the Illustration Class, I think we ought to get together and contribute something toward a sort of. . . ."

"Souvenir, Cynthia?"

"Memorial, Cyn?"

"Consolation prize? Reward of Merit?"

"Oh shush!" Cynthia, trying not to giggle, held up an admonitory hand. "Has anybody got any suggestions, any real, sensible ones I mean? Henry's taught our class for at least twenty of his twenty five years here——"

"Nineteen." Judy corrected.

"Nineteen then. But as to what we can give him, I haven't the faintest idea. Have you?"

Amid the shower of suggestions that followed, "An alarm clock, to get him to class on time, so we won't have to wait till midnight for a crit. . . ." "A box . . . a *crate* of charcoal all his own, so he won't break ours. . . ." "A new tie, that purple one of his offends my aesthetic sense. . . ." Berieth's voice sounded, clear and unamused.

"How much can we afford to give, apiece?" Berieth was invariably practical.

Nancy, sitting on the magazine table, slim silk-stockinged legs swinging like twin pendulums, suggested brightly, "How about giving two dollars apiece? We could get something quite nice for that, couldn't we? And I move that Cynthia Wanstead be appointed head of a committee of three to discover what Henry would like, because we don't want to give something that's perfectly useless to the poor dear."

There was a faint murmur through the

darkening class room. The class, by a scribbled notice on the board, had been kept after the model's last pose for this very meeting. Nancy, just rounding her first month as a full fledged illustration student, looked about her and felt suddenly, vaguely, uncomfortable. Chick's quiet face was blank and rather set, Judy flushed scarlet, was biting her lip. Cynthia was frowning slightly, Nancy wondered what was wrong? Shouldn't she have suggested Cynthia as head of the committee? Which had been wrong, her suggestion, or that she, the newest member of the class, had made it?

The pause lasted not more than half an awkward minute, then Judy, always the quickest in the class, was on her feet.

"I second the motion with regard to Miss Wanstead, and suggest that Chick and Miss Brewster be the other members. As Nancy's mother is a friend of Henry's, it's my idea that she can find out, sort of informally, what Henry would like. And she'd be least liable to be suspected."

"Hear! Hear!" came various approving voices, and the awkward moment had passed.

"And furthermore," continued Judy, still on her feet, "I suggest that we put a shoebox, with a slit in it, behind the big drawing board, and that you drop your contributions in that, anonymously. Those of you who can't pay now, can put in a promise to pay a little later. But do give all you can, please."

The meeting ended in gay suggestions, some quite practical, some distinctly weird, as to what Henry's present should be, and twilight, which came early these snowy winter days, was shutting down as they straggled, laughing and talking, into the brightly lighted hallway.

Nancy blinked in the glare. She still felt a little huffy over that awkward pause after her remark, and was still wondering what the trouble could have been. Cynthia behind her asked:

"I'm coming your way, Nancy. Want to give me a lift in your luxury-liner?" The big car always called for Nancy on its way to pick up her father each evening. The Brewsters were living in the country this winter, a half hour's drive out.

"Sure, come along, honey. There's plenty of time, we'll take you clear home." Once in the car she could find out what she had done that was wrong.

But Cynthia had, apparently asked for the ride for that very reason. "You know, Nancy," she began tactfully, "you sort of put your foot in it this afternoon. . . ."

"Oh gosh, I guessed that! But I haven't any idea how."

"No? Really? I thought you knew."

Nancy shook her head and in the glow of a passing street light could see Cynthia's quick, inquiring glance. When she spoke her explanation came as a total surprise.

"It was that two dollar business. How many of the kids do you suppose could afford two dollars? Elsie works like a dog for the eight dollars a week she pays for room and board, Chick doesn't get a cent for his monitor job, he has to earn whatever he spends outside, Judy gets a tiny allowance from home, and not always that, and I get the munificent sum of a dollar a week, but have to piece out my lunches from that. I imagine that most of us could scrape up just about a quarter apiece."

"Oh, I am so sorry," cried Nancy, thoroughly overwhelmed by her unconscious tactlessness. "But—just two dollars!" It still seemed an amazingly small sum. "Why, I get ten a week from Mother for expenses. . . ."

"I know you do. Somethin' scandalous for a little girl of your age." Cynthia spoke lightly, "But when you come to earn that much, you'll know a bit more about the worth of ten dollars. Here's where I live. 'Bye!"

The feeling of soreness, of being just a little bit abused, persisted all the next day. Everytime that somebody whispered behind Nancy's back, everytime that she passed a group that seemed suddenly to stop talking, she fancied they were discussing her and her tactlessness. But by afternoon this had faded somewhat. Nancy was too jolly, too well liked, too sane and well balanced to build up a fancied grievance, and there were no real grounds for her belief. In fact she was, herself, feeling a little hard up just now; she could just manage the change for lunch, but her contribution to Henry's box, the one Judy had tacked up in an inconspicuous corner behind the big drawing board, must wait till Monday, when her allowance was due.

As always it lay beside her plate, one of Dad's checks in a long envelope, at breakfast on Monday morning. And on the first day of the month the bank was always open till seven o'clock, so Nancy slipped the envelope into her purse to take to school. She could borrow the change for lunch, returning it tomorrow when her check had been cashed.

Mother hadn't come down to breakfast so Nancy ran upstairs to the top-floor studio to say good-bye. Mrs. Brewster, in paint smock over her pyjamas, absently returned Nancy's kiss and patted her cheek. Nancy knew that she had just received a long detective serial to illustrate for one of the big magazines, and was wrapped in the first fine frenzy of creation. Mother didn't want to be talked to when these moods were on so Nancy didn't attempt conversation.

The afternoon model was a good one this week and at four o'clock Nancy reluctantly put away her charcoal and drawing board, slipped out of her smock to hang it in her locker. Cynthia, whose place for the week had been just behind her, looked up from tacking a new sheet on her board.

"Not much luck today," she reported. "I'll start a fresh drawing tomorrow. A new dress, chicken?"

Nancy glanced down, somewhat disparagingly at the pretty, leaf brown silk dress she wore. "Oh goodness, no. It's awfully old. Wish I had something new for Henry's presentation party next week. And by the way, I haven't put my money in the box yet, but I'm cashing a check tonight and I'll bring it tomorrow."

Cynthia nodded. "That's all right, Judy thought she wouldn't collect it till Thursday, give the class plenty of time. Going home in the car?"

Nancy shook her head. "No, I've got an errand or two first, I told Adolph to pick me up at Dad's office at five o'clock. Besides the walk will do me good," and she tore through the swing door, down the long hall to the cloak-room. Today was a nice day, the start on the afternoon sketch had been a good one, and, as she scurried out into the street, there was a pleasant feeling of snow in the air. A *nice* day!

The wind behind seemed to add wings to her heels, she snuggled a nose, already rosy with the cold, into the high collar of her smart little Persian lamb coat, and smiled out, happily, at other wind blown shoppers hurrying home. The bank wasn't far, just a few blocks, and Dad's office just beyond that. Nancy paused a moment to gaze at some etchings in a print shop window, at a bit of jade and lapis behind the shining plate glass at Gambols, then again caught up by the wind was hustled along to the next block. Here for a moment the wind died down. Nancy, pausing for an instant to catch her breath gazed straight ahead, straight into the eyes of Esmerelda who wore The Green Dress.

Esmerelda was truly a highbrow, in fact her brow seemed to extend far back into the curves and undulations of her silver hair. Her nose was long, and narrow, her eyes under their lacquered lids drooped coyly and her mouth was a mere splotch of paint, rose madder, if the truth be told. Nancy giggled and drew nearer, fascinated.

Esmerelda stood full in the glare of the hundred watt globes and displayed, that all passers-by might behold and envy, The Green Dress. It had big puffy sleeves with a line of delicate black embroidery from shoulder to cuff, and the same motif was repeated around the bottom of the ducky little basque bodice. The soft sash of rough, crepe silk repeated the line of the soft black tie that draped about Esmerelda's white porcelain throat, and the whole confection fastened on the shoulder with a button of carved green stained wood. Nancy flattened her nose against the chilled pane and gazed, entranced. Esmerelda smirked back.

"Pooh!" scoffed Nancy. "Betcha' I'd look better in that than you!"

"Bet'cha wouldn't!" simpered Esmerelda.

At which challenge Nancy wheeled and marched through the wide swing door. Just, of course, to show Esmerelda.

The dress, so the salesgirl told her, was a Paris original, but because of its unusual size, a fourteen, and because of the midseason sales, was marked at a price positively ridiculous in its moderation. Not bothering to ask the sum,

Nancy just slipped into one of the bright, little silver and gray cells to try it on, to see if she could rival Esmerelda in the gown. Then on the tips of her toes twirled triumphantly before the triple mirror.

"Ah . . ha, Esmerelda," she murmured to herself. "I told you so!"

And indeed the dress was becoming. "Nay, it is ravishing," murmured Nancy in person to Nancy in the glass. "My dear, you'll knock 'em all cold."

"Not a single alteration," confirmed the salesgirl.

"How much?" asked Nancy, suddenly going all practical.

"Forty-five dollars," remarked the salesgirl casually, as though one were remarking, "Forty-five cents," and added brightly, "You could wear it home, just as it is and I'll send the other if you like. It is lovely on you."

Nancy considered the situation. "I've got a check here," she began and took it out of her purse, "I was just on my way to the bank to cash it. See if they'll take it, and . . . you can hold the dress till I get the other five." This reluctantly. She did want to take the green frock home, right from under the supercilious eye of Esmerelda.

The salesgirl departed. Nancy, standing in the doorway of the gray and silver cell and still clad in the green confection, saw her conferring with a gentleman in correct black cutaway, natty gray striped trousers, with a white carnation in his buttonhole. Presently he bent a shiny black head and made a brief notation on the slip which the salesgirl held out to him. In a moment she returned.

"It's all right," she reported. "You can take it right as it is, and the check will be sufficient. We can bill your father for the remainder."

"I'll stop in and pay the rest, myself, in a few days," Nancy decided, and only on the sales-girl's insistence did she consent to take the dress home with her. Oh the lovely, lovely green. Nancy stroked it happily before she took it off. At least she could forego the wearing of it until it was completely hers. She went out with a silver and gray box under her arm and turned to smile triumphantly at Esmerelda, standing im-modestly forlorn in a plain white rayon slip, beneath the hundred watt globes. Then some-body pulled a curtain and the window was lost to sight.

On the trip home she debated the question of that additional five dollars, and of course, a little something extra to carry her through the month. There was Henry's present, too, and that must be settled tomorrow. Right after dinner she took the gray and silver box up to the studio where Mother had returned to work.

When a serial first came Mrs. Brewster labored early and late on it until she had, as she called it, got into the mood. After that it went more easily.

Now she looked up with a little absent-minded frown as Nancy took the shining green silk out of the tissue wrappings.

Nancy was beginning to have a slight, unexplainable uneasiness about that dress. Perhaps she shouldn't have been quite so impulsive, quite so willing to take the dare of the haughty Esmerelda. "Mother," she stammered, "I'm sorry, I didn't have quite enough to pay for this. . . ."

Mrs. Brewster laid down the pencil with which she was checking the illustratable points in the typewritten manuscript on her knee and ran a hand through her dark curly bob. "Now, Nancy," she stated firmly, "this has got to stop. You don't seem to have the slightest idea of the value of money. How much do you owe for this dress?"

"Only five dollars," protested the apologetic Nancy in a muffled voice, "but Mother, you can take it out of my next month's allowance."

"And today is the first," reminded Mrs. Brewster. "What are you going to do for your lunches the rest of the month? You certainly can't expect to sponge on Cynthia and Julia. They have all they can do without feeding you, Nancy."

Nancy wriggled uncomfortably. "But Mother. . . ."

"No, I'm sorry, Nancy. I'm afraid this is one time I shall have to be firm. You must take the dress back. I know it's very pretty, and it was undoubtedly a bargain, but you had a new one only three weeks ago. I'm sorry darling, but that's how I feel about it."

Nancy's own feelings, as she left the studio

could scarcely bear expression. Down in her own room she shook out the folds of the green silk. No, she couldn't take it back, though at the moment she hated the dress. But she couldn't, somehow, summon up the courage to march back and say . . . what could she say . . . that Mother hadn't liked it . . . that she had made a mistake . . . that . . . that. . . . Oh dear, what did one say when one took things back to the store? Why, it didn't seem honest, somehow, to buy a thing and then return it.

It also wouldn't be honest to sponge on Judy and Cynthia and Berieth and the others, for her lunches till the first of next month. There seemed nothing left to do but to earn that remaining five dollars, in some way, and enough besides to carry her through to the first. Nancy thoughtfully folded the green dress and put it away. She would keep to her decision at least, and not wear it until it was all paid for.

The problem was still on her mind when she slipped into the car beside Dad the next morning. Dad always read the paper on his way into town, and Nancy often took a book along for the half-hour ride through too familiar suburban streets. But today her eyes caught sight of the half of the paper Dad discarded. She folded it into a flat parcel and when she left the car at the Academy door, it was with her purse and the new box of charcoal she had brought from the studio. With the paper still beneath her arm she slapped open the door to the illustration room, nodded good mornings right and left and found a quiet place in a deserted corner behind the high, easel blackboard. Here she opened it up.

"Help Wanted" was in large letters across the top of the closely printed columns. That, thought Nancy with satisfaction, was exactly what she wanted. Now where would she be liable to find a list of the things she could do? "Domestic Servants." Hardly that. "Stenographers." Darn, that took training. "Waitresses." Nancy shook her light brown curls. She'd be sure to be missed at dinner if she tried a thing like that, and besides, all those heavy trays. Nancy was looking for something light and simple, suited to the daughter of a famous artist and a noted editor. But there didn't seem to be anything today that just suited her needs.

"Sales Help Wanted." Nancy pondered over that one. Could she possibly go from door to door saying, "Madame, I am the Fuller Brush man. . . ." She giggled to herself, then felt slightly discouraged. Oh dear, how *did* one find a job anyway?

Then in a tiny place, just two or three lines near the bottom of a column she found what she wanted—a heading "Artists Wanted."

The first ad was useless. It was from Gambles, the big department store and they wanted Artists, to do wash drawings for catalog work. But the second one seemed more encouraging.

"Artists Wanted, Girls to color Christmas, Easter, Valentine cards. Apply nine to five." And the address followed.

Nancy cut out the tiny notice with her silver pen knife and slipped it into her purse, then she crossed the room and chucked the remainder of the paper into the waste basket.

"Rest!" called Chick, the monitor, to the model. Nancy glanced at the clock. Ten thirty. If she went right out now she might get the job today, start earning money immediately this very morning.

That was one nice thing about Art School, she thought later as she hurried along Base Street. You don't have to keep special hours, or report on where you were going or where you had been. The Academy treated you like an adult, and you were on your own responsibility.

The address was not far away, twenty minutes walk, and today Nancy wasn't wasting any money on taxicabs and such. The number was one of a row of ancient, slightly down-at-heel brick houses, and a small showcase beside the door advertised the name "S. Greenschmidt," beneath it. "Greeting Cards for Every Occasion." Nancy glanced at the dusty, gaudily tinted cards that leaned haphazardly behind the streaked glass, then pushed open the door. An arrow pointed the way ahead. Down the passage was another door and a bell jangled remotely as she went through it.

Behind a tall counter in a small dingy room were stacks and stacks of gray bound books, all just alike, and one, spread open upon the counter showed that they were salsemen's samples.

Nancy, waiting, idly turned the leaves. There were greeting cards of every description, and for every possible occasion. She noticed that many of them were printed in black on white cards with the color later filled in by hand. Was this the type of work she would be expected to do?

Then a woman waddled in and Nancy glanced up. The woman wore a dress of faded black beneath a soiled black smock, much stained down the side as though she had wiped her brushes on it. Her hand too, with the fat fingers and pointed nails was discolored on the forefinger. Her pudgy face bulged in the cheeks, like a chipmunk trying to carry two nuts at once, beneath hair of glittering bottle-blond.

"Was there something Miss——" she asked.

Nancy suppressing a frantic desire to turn and bolt murmured, "I—I came about your advertisement in the paper this morning."

"You mean . . ." the woman's eyes took in the little Persian lamb coat with its big fox collar, the smart gloves and bag, the Paris hat.

"You advertised for girls to color cards," Nancy reminded her.

"Oh yes," the woman stopped smiling. "Haf you had any experience?"

"I'm—I'm an art student," admitted Nancy.

The woman sniffed loudly. "We've had them before, they ain't much good, I can tell you, dearie. What's a nice girl like you want to work for?"

"I need the money," Nancy stated flatly, but at the woman's caustic, "Oh, I see," felt as though she were suspected of picking pockets, and wanted the job to replace her ill gotten gains.

"Well," said the woman finally. "I'll call Pa. *Pa!*" she raised her voice in a shrill shout that started footsteps in the back of the shop. "C'mon out. Here's a girl for you to see."

The man who shuffled through the doorway had features that amusingly exaggerated his daughter's, his faded eyes peered from behind a pair of bent, steel-bowed spectacles; his suit covered, like hers, by a paint-stained smock.

"Wants a job, does she?" he asked, surveying the uncomfortable Nancy from hat to gloves. "Art student? Well, now, I tell you Miss, we ain't had much luck with art students," and then as Nancy's face so plainly showed her disappointment, "but I tell you what, if you want to, you can work here for the rest of the day and my daughter here'll look over your work. If it's good enough you can come back tomorrow."

"Oh, that's nice," cried the relieved Nancy. There was no doubt that the trial would be successful. Why Mother was one of the best illustrators in the country, and she herself, had made, so they said, amazing progress in her first year at the Academy.

Full of confidence now, she followed Miss Greenschmidt through the door behind the counter and down another hallway where she was directed to hang up her hat and coat. "I'll lend you a smock for today," the woman told her. "Now you'll need a number two water color brush, and paints, red and green to start with, later on gold and silver. Let's see," she figured with a stump of a pencil on the back of a card, "that'll be eighty cents, want to pay for it, or shall I take it out of what you do?"

Nancy considered that she must still buy her own lunch and suggested that the latter course might be advisable. The woman nodded doubtfully, and led her down a long, well lighted but dingy room to a deal table at the end. There were a dozen or more such tables in the room and at each one five or six girls worked, talking softly.

A very self conscious Nancy waited while the

woman went out and returned with a pack of white cards which she placed on the table.

"Now these are easy,' she explained. "We pay a half cent apiece for these because there's only two colors in them. See, the green wreath and the red bell."

The card bore the message "Christmas Joy!" and a sketch of two children, one in a green suit, the other in red rompers, tying up a big red bell inside a green wreath. Miss Greenschmidt showed her how to do the first one. The fat hands, surprisingly deft and swift, loaded the brush with the required color and filled in a card in a half minute, by Nancy's little wrist watch. Then she was left alone to start work by herself.

Before her was a glass of paint water, her pile of cards, a saucer on which to mix the colors to the required consistency. With some feeling of excitement, since this was her very first job and she had obtained it alone, without outside pull, Nancy plunged into work. She had a big table to herself, so there was plenty of room to spread the red painted cards to dry. Once those were done she would go back and put in the greens.

The first cards went very slowly. The outlines were difficult to follow and Nancy's own style was what Henry described as "delightfully loose and free" but scarcely adapted to the coloring of greeting cards. The small pile of finished work grew with a speed scarcely discernible to the naked eye.

But after a while she began to catch the trick, the particular flick of the wrist that fitted a loaded brush into the green wreath. The curve of the hand that accommodated itself to the shaping of a red bell, monotonous and tiring, because you must watch, carefully, every outline, became easier with practice. All down the room the other girls were busy on similar piles of white cards, and when Miss Greenschmidt had left the room, pleasant laughter, little jests and comments spread from table to table. One might even get to like this place a little, and after a long time, thought Nancy.

A half hour of work, which seemed at least an hour and the woman returned to inspect what Nancy had done. She counted eighteen, threw out six. "And a quarter each for those you spoil," she said. "Two of these is dark, three haf gone over the line, one has a spot on it."

After that she worked more slowly and the next half hour's batch, while it was only thirteen, passed with only one thrown out." The woman nodded. "All right, we can use you I guess," she said. "The bell for lunch rings in ten minutes. You'll be back after noon?"

"Oh yes, thank you," Nancy's arms ached from the unaccustomed and monotonous movements, she'd be glad to stand up and stretch, and she was ravenously hungry. She spent the next ten minutes planning a particularly delicious luncheon, though she knew that the few coins left in her purse would probably limit her to beef stew and a glass of milk.

It turned out to be just that, with a chocolate bar to munch on the way back to the shop, and by half past twelve she had plunged into work again. By two-thirty she had finished the Christmas Joys and Miss Greenschmidt came round to inspect them, nodded, counted out two that were faulty, and brought her a new batch. These were valentines and were prettier. They called for gold paint, as well as the red, and a tube of yellow which the woman charged to her account. Nancy thought ruefully that her work today would scarcely pay for her material, but was cheered by the information that the valentines paid better; two for five cents because they were more difficult and, of course, took longer.

They were indeed much slower, but the change in design was a pleasant break in the monotony. Slowly the new pile grew smaller, the finished stack a little higher. Nancy leaning back to yawn and stretch caught the eye of a girl at the next table and grinned back cheerily. Ou . . . f, but she was weary! What time was it? Three-thirty already? In another twenty minutes the crowd from the Art Academy would begin to trickle through the big iron studded doors. She must leave in time to meet Adolph with the car, and tomorrow she could give him some excuse to come a little later.

That night she fell sound asleep in the car and slept all the long ride out to Rose Valley. Dad didn't waken her till they had arrived at the house. But Nancy remembered that she had heard that the first day on a new job was always the hardest.

The next morning, complete with her own

smock, she was ready and on the job by nine o'clock. Today she meant to earn more than mere lunch money. The morning went quite well and she finished off the valentines and was given a slip saying that she had made a dollar and twenty cents. Out of that, however, had to come the eighty cents for her first supplies, twenty-five more for yellow, ten for gilt, and then for those cards she had spoiled. Nancy eyed it dubiously. This was rather like the frog jumping to get out of the well, three leaps backward every time he made two forward!

She had borrowed a quarter from Adolph for lunch today. She gulped down the meal and scurried back to the Academy in the few minutes she had saved. She must, simply must get a whiff of charcoal and turpentine, a glimpse of the dingy, sketch-plastered walls or she couldn't, for sheer homesickness, stick it out all the remainder of the long tiresome afternoon.

Softly she swung open the door to the illustration class and peeked in. The model was a girl in warm brown, with a wide hat of yellow straw and a great sheaf of autumn leaves in her arms, all against a background of dingy, pale corn color. Nancy's glance took in Cynthia, who was just starting a water color; Judy's strong study in oils; Chick's charcoal sketch, already the best in the room, and for a moment she wavered in her determination to keep on with her job. The model seemed quite the nicest, the light the pleasantest and today the possibility of making a masterpiece seemed the surest of the entire year.

With a sigh she let the door swing shut behind her, hurried out to the street and back towards the job. Somehow work wasn't all the glorious, interesting things she had imagined it would be and she didn't feel half as independent as she had expected to feel. But perhaps if she worked very hard, all the afternoon, she could make enough for her contribution to Henry's gift box.

For the afternoon there was another batch of the "Christmas Joys." The swing of them came more easily today and mechanically her brush followed the curves of the bell, sloshed color on the wreaths as minute by minute the pile grew before her. About half past three she indulged herself in a small vacation; she took time off to count the cards she had done. There were almost two dollars' worth, with those she had finished in the morning, and a nice job too, neat and all tidily inside the printed outlines.

When Miss Greenschmidt came, about four o'clock one could tell immediately by the tones of her voice that she was in a bad temper. One poor little girl was told, in strident tones, to pack up and get out of here, she was no use, no use at all. Nancy feeling awfully sorry for her, was pleasantly complacent about her own afternoon's task.

Miss Greenschmidt, now at Nancy's table, picked up the neat little stack of colored cards and flipped them over swiftly. She wasn't putting any aside this time, that was a good sign, then Nancy looked up, smiling. Her smile stopped. For just an instant her heart seemed also to stop, then she thought consolingly, "well, she can't *eat* me, anyhow!" Miss Greenschmidt's brow was black with thunder, her mouth a curved down half moon of fury. She slammed the cards to the table so that the glass of water jumped half an inch, spilling into a little colored pool. With one soiled finger she pointed directly at Nancy.

"You—you—!" she sputtered, "you come in here with your fancy fur coat and your fancy ways . . . and spoil my cards! I gif you work. . . . I take work from my goot girls to gif to you! Now you get oudt, *get oudt* already and quick!"

"But— but—" stammered the astonished Nancy, "what's the matter with the cards?" All down the long room the girls had stopped working, pausing to look up, to crane forward and see what was happening. It was amazingly silent.

Without speaking Miss Greenschmidt spread the cards fanwise, that Nancy might see, they were all alike, not too badly done, she thought. She should have a couple of dollars' work there.

"Look! You look!" quavered the enraged woman, pounding her palm down on the little pile of cards. "Look here." She slipped one from the pack, Nancy's pack, another of the same pattern from her pocket and slapped them down together.

Nancy gaped. Oh my goodness!

For the past three hours she had been painting red wreaths and green bells instead of green wreaths and red bells, as in the sample.

"I'm so sorry," apologized Nancy, rising in her best behaved, little-girl manner. "You can of course take it out of my money——"

"Money? You get no money! And what's more, you don't leaf this place till you pay me for the cards you haf spoiled."

"But I can't do that," Nancy protested, remembering the few remaining coins in her purse.

"You can leaf—," the woman's eyes roved over Nan's hair, her dress, her shoes, her paint stained hands, "you can leaf that ring," she nodded her head in satisfaction. "You leaf that. I gif you paper, when you haf the money, you come back, I give you the ring then."

Nancy looked down, doubtfully, at the pretty ring. It was a large, old fashioned thing of clustered garnets and tiny pearls which Mother had brought her from France. Oh well, perhaps it was all right, if the woman would actually give her a receipt for it. "Well," agreed

Nancy with a brief sigh. "But——"

"Then you get right out, I don't want no more of this work from you, young lady."

Nancy walked silently toward the door. Now she must get her hat, get her coat, get completely away from this terrible place before she started to cry. Because now her nose tickled alarmingly, and her throat was strangely tight. One mustn't cry in front of Miss Greenschmidt.

But once on the street she felt so relieved to be away from the whole Greenschmidt tribe, away from the monotony of coloring cards and free once more to return to the illustration class and all its bright chatter and pleasant work-a-day atmosphere, that her brief career slipped from her with scarcely a pang of regret for its death.

Scuttering through the chill bracing dusk, down Base street, Nancy Brewster, erstwhile wage-earner firmly faced Nancy Brewster, the rather spoiled daughter of the famous Carol

Heywood, and told her a plain fact or two.

"Here," said Nancy one to Nancy two, "is where you start to get a little sense under your hat. No more of this 'pound foolish' stuff for you, Miss Brewster. You put your silly pride in your pocket and take Esmerelda's green dress back to the store tomorrow. Then get your ring out of hock, and put a fat five dollars, by way of penance, into Henry's gift-box. And after that, well I guess you'd better put aside a little every month towards the rainy day when you really have to look for a job. Judging by this sample, you'll need it!"

As head of the Detection department for the Committee on buying-Henry-a-present, Nancy came in on Friday with the report that Mr. Henry had greatly admired some very lovely old firedogs now in Todhunter's window. This had come via Nancy's mother, who had been admitted to the secret.

So a hurried meeting of the committee was called—Judy, with the box of money; Chick, as class monitor; Cynthia, as head of the committee, and of course Nancy.

"The question before the house," announced Cynthia, "is, have we got enough money?" How much are these firedogs?"

"I've phoned Todhunter's already," reported Judy, "and we've got within two dollars of it, but two dollars is two dollars!"

For a moment Nancy thought wildly of offering to make up the extra, or of pretending that she had forgotten to put in her own contribution, but immediately rejected that idea; she had learned quite a lot in the past week. Perhaps there was an even better way.

"Maybe if I went to Mr. Todhunter himself, and told him what we were buying the things for, and that the illustration class of the Art Academy had honored his shop by selecting something from his window," only half seriously she made the suggestion, "why he'd give us a special price."

"Good girl!" applauded Chick, and Cynthia beamed. "Say, I bet he'd do just that. Why it's a grand idea. When can you see him?"

"Right now," decided Nancy. "I haven't got anything ready for criticism this week," and she jumped up and started down the hallway toward the cloakroom, then turned back. "Judy, just what is Todhunter's address? Have you got it? Good, I'll copy it down now."

As she opened her purse to take out a little silver pencil, something fluttered to the floor. Cynthia, bending to retrieve the small, newspaper clipping, couldn't help but read it, then handed it back.

"I'm sorry," she said. But she looked awfully surprised for an instant. Then she exclaimed, "Gracious, child, what are you doing with that?

I thought every art student in town knew that Greenschmidt woman, the ad has been in for the past year."

It was Nancy's turn to look surprised, "Should I have known her, I never thought to ask anyone. But . . . well," she started to laugh, "I know her now, all right, I worked there for two days . . . or almost."

"Two days!" Chick and Judy joined the astonished and admiring chorus, and Cynthia burst out with, "I only stuck it for half a day. Odious person!"

"But," Nancy's voice was demure, "I left, owing her money."

"You're telling me," grinned Cynthia, but her voice held approval. "Young woman, two days for an art student is an all world, all time record. You should have a medal!"

CHAPTER V

# *Artist's Model*

THE swing doors of the illustration class slapped violently and the busy class, as one man, looked up frowning at the interruption, an unrepentant Nancy, curls dancing, toes scarcely able to stay on the ground, waved a thick yellow envelope.

"It's a job. J-O-B. Job!" The envelope fanned the air and her voice squeaked with excitement.

"A *job!* Nancy darling . . . can I just touch the envelope to bring me luck! Boy! Our Nancy's got a job!" Tones of awe and amazement that the class baby should be the first to land a story to illustrate. But then of course, as Eve remarked somewhat chillingly, the class baby's mother was Carol Heywood, herself a famous illustrator.

Nancy admitted unblushingly that it was mother who had steered the job her way. "She said she thought I ought to get some practical experience, and the editor of *Weekly Stories* said it was okay with him if I'd get it done early enough to find someone else to do it, in case mine weren't good enough."

The model, perched high and uncomfortably on the model stand, noting that her class had deserted, came out of her pose.

Someone had opened the envelope, was flipping through the pages. "Love in-a-Mist, by Carlton Ross. Yes, he's a good writer. He-and-she-stuff." . . . the illustrator's term for a love story.

"It came in the morning's mail." Nancy explained to whoever stopped talking long enough to hear her.

"What's this, what's this!" Chick, the class monitor, had been out in the corridor setting his palette with fresh paint. "I turn my back five seconds and the room sounds like the Zoo's prize monkey house."

"But Nancy's got a Job!" By now it was almost a chorus, a chant.

"Well, what of it!" But you could see he too was impressed. "Wait till rest period to talk about it, can't you? And you," he wheeled on Nancy, blond brows beetling above twinkling eyes. "Beat it with that manuscript. Take it back to the rest room and read it."

Discipline of a sort was restored. Nancy beat it. Chuckling, she curled on the top step of the rest room stairway where she could look down over the antique room with its plaster busts of dead and gone Greeks, and its patient, plodding little would-be artists. Pathetic, they were. She felt sorry for them, not having the job *she* had. But they'd get their thrills, every one of them in time. Someone paused at the foot of the steps and gazed up. Cynthia. Behind her, grinning sheepishly, Judy.

"We came to see what a real job looks like," they explained, perching below her.

So Nancy read the first typed page of the manuscript and passed it down, page by page, to the others. Pretty soon she took a stump of a pencil out of her smock pocket. "Here's a place that might illustrate well." She checked it on the side. "Mother always marks her stories as she reads them through, then when she's finished she picks out the four or five best places and makes her composition studies from those."

Judy nodded, interested. "It certainly helps to be born into an artist's family, Nancy." And when she'd finished the final page, Cynthia asked, "How many drawings can you have? And what are you going to do with them?"

"We . . . ll," Nancy considered, the point of her pencil denting a dimple. "I can have one big one, and a 'spot' that's a head or something, and ought to be the heroine. Then for the big one I thought the place where the heroine waits on the park bench and the two children go by with the goat cart. That'd make a honey. But I'll have to go out and sketch a park bench."

"*And* a wagon," said Cynthia.

"And a *goat*," said Judy. "And of course your heroine. Though that's a mere trifle!"

"Oh any girl in the class will pose for you," volunteered Cynthia for the class. "Eve'd jump at the chance. And there's a couple of park benches down near the station." Verisimilitude was important in this illustration business.

Nancy was already scribbling little arrangements of goat, wagon, park bench and girl on a page of her sketch book. "Mmm. Haven't much time, he wants it in two weeks."

"But the *goat?*" persisted Judy.

Cynthia, hugging her knees, had an idea. "When Pierson gave us 'city streets' for the composition class last week, I went down to Third and Walnut. Back of it somewhere there's a funny old junk shop, and next to it a broken down board fence around a vacant lot. There's a goat in there."

Nancy bounced on her step. "You're an angel. Once I get the goat, the wagon will be easy."

Thereafter for some days she was intensely occupied with compositions; those little sketches, a few inches square which every artist makes before he sets to work on the larger drawing, really a sort of shorthand note of lights and shades, arrangements of shapes and figures meaning as yet nothing to anyone but the artist himself. Scribbling them in the car as she drove home at night with Dad, leaping out of bed to snatch paper and pencil and jot down just the perfect composition which had flashed before her eyes as she began to drop asleep, scrawling them on the backs of envelopes in the Academy lunch room. Judy offered advice. Cynthia's opinion was asked, Chick was called into consultation, till the whole illustration class had had its say.

"You want a heavier, darker group there, to hold down your values against the type on the page," advised Elsie Dinsmore seriously. His own work was solid with blacks.

"Something not so heavy, Nancy dear. Your style doesn't fit it," drawled Eve.

"A little flippancy in the treatment," was Chick's idea. "The story's a light one, don't go all solemn over it."

"I think that particular magazine takes its authors rather importantly," said Cynthia. And Nancy began to feel she had a non-stop ticket on a merry-go-round. This wasn't getting her anywhere at all.

And then Cynthia advised. "Chuck *all* this advice, even this if you want to. But for Pete's sake, honey, get on with your drawing. Your time is getting short, and you can't hand a bunch of rough comps to an editor."

"I guess you're right," murmured Nancy with rare meekness, gazing blankly at a pile of sketches almost as thick as the manuscript. "But . . ." wavering. "But I can't seem to make up my mind. Would you . . . ?"

"Stop it!" commanded Cynthia sharply. "You're getting the jitters. Pick out the half dozen you like best, shut your eyes and *grab*."

And by such unorthodox method did Nancy choose the composition for her first job.

Eve had been thrilled at the idea of posing. But the afternoon she was needed she was so sorry, but somehow she had matinee tickets and "wouldn't tomorrow, Nancy dear, do just as well?" Nancy let her go, and Judy took her place. That wasn't difficult; any smart, pretty girl, on a park bench in the springtime, looking as though she were waiting for the hero of the story, would have done. It was the goat that bothered her; she must, she kept telling herself, get that goat drawing. But still the days sped by and she postponed it.

And then it began to rain. For three days it rained without ceasing. For three mornings Nancy, clad in raincoat and rubbers, went off to school, vowing that *that* afternoon she'd go out and find the goat.

"Only I can't," she mourned, "work with an umbrella over my head," gazing at the downpour sluicing along the studio skylight.

The moment the rain let up Cynthia ordered her out. "Get it done with and come back and be our little sunbeam again!"

"Yes'm." murmured Nancy, moving slowly towards the door. But just as it swung shut behind her, "Slave driver!" she flung over her shoulder, and heard the class laugh behind her.

Yes, the class had been sweet about this job of hers, treating it as though it were a class job, taking such a pride in it, in the fact that someone of them had turned professional, bragging about it so to the sculptors and painters. She had heard even Chick say to Parrish, one of the older portrait class, "Well, anyway, it's a real *job!*" And Judy had left her own work, to pose tirelessly, and others had helped with the tree background, had brought clippings of goat wagons, photographs of small boys, had given tireless criticisms. Nancy sighed. A bit wearing, to feel that the reputation of the illustration class rested on her shoulders even temporarily. Still, they'd all been such *dears* about it.

The rain held up as she paddled down Market to Third, found the junk shop which she identified from Cynthia's sketch of it, and beyond it the boards of the vacant lot. A hole where two boards were put. She crouched down and crawled through. Hurray! There was the goat, complete with two horns, a perky tail, flappy ears and the usual cynical expression. As she stood regarding the creature thoughtfully, it began to rain again.

Nancy opened her umbrella. The goat, impervious to inclement weather, chewed thoughtfully. Oh dear, what to do now! If she went back and told the class she hadn't drawn the goat yet. . . . But she couldn't juggle an umbrella, a sketch book and a pencil. Besides the creature had turned his back!

Perhaps if she could find the animal's owner they would take him indoors for her.

Beyond the goat, at the back of the lot was a

little brick house. Its back door was open hospitably. Nancy picked her way over stones and rubbish and mounted the steps. There she hesitated a moment. But she'd have to get this goat somehow, it was, she giggled to herself, beginning to get her own.

A frowsey hallway showed doors on either side. At the first she knocked. Scuffling of footsteps within, the door opened a crack. Two white eyeballs rolled up from a small brown face, gazed at her solemnly then the head turned and a stentorian whisper carried to someone back in the room.

"White lady for to see you, Mammy!"

Heavier footsteps, the door was flung open, a wide and cheerful negro mammy, head bound in a bright cloth, beamed hospitably.

"I wanted to ask about that goat out there," began Nancy, wondering how to put her strange request. "Is he yours? Would you be willing to let me borrow him for a while? I'm an art student from the Academy and I want to make his picture."

The wide ginghamed bulk shook with cheerful laughter. "Why sho' honey. Jes go right ahead and make your picture. He won't bite you. Come in now. . . ."

Nancy entered. Dinner was steaming on the stove, a pleasant smell of coffee in the air, another small boy in tattered knickers and sweater sat on the coal box. Just sitting. The room was cluttered with furniture, an overstuffed and much abused sofa, three great chairs ditto, a huge dining room table, a wash tub in active service. Hopeless to carry out her idea of bringing the goat in here to sketch, there just wasn't room for him. But how about hiring him with his owners for the afternoon, and taking him over to the Academy?

"She want' to *hire* Ambrose," repeated the

younger child in a tone of surprise, but Willyum understood. He'd seen a lady drawing a picture of that there junk shop round the corner, he'd asked some questions. Yes *sir*, if anybody wanted a picture of their Ambrose he was all *for* it, and proceeded to collect caps, coats, and the goat.

A strange procession, Nancy leading, trim in blue raincoat, blue beret and blue umbrella. Behind her, one eager small boy tugging on a rope, one full sized goat, displaying extreme reluctance to be tugged, one small boy shoving on the same animal.

Nancy was juggling with plans. How did one insert a goat, together with two ragged small boys, through the staid corridors of the Art Academy? At the front door Tom stood guard, brave in brass buttons and blue serge, friend to all the students, but certainly no admitter of goats, whether required in illustrations or otherwise. And there was Miss Bennet too, at the desk. The thing to do, decided Nancy, was to try the back door, where crated and boxed exhibitions were unpacked amid a not displeasing disarray of old boards, nails and odd packing materials.

They circled the block and approaching the Cherry Street entrance, Nancy motioned the procession to wait. She tripped up the steps. The back door was open, but, oh bitter blow, the iron grill was closed. She could look into the hall but not enter, and if she rang Tom would be the one to answer.

Then she saw a familiar form cross the hallway beyond the grill.

"Chick!" she called. "Hey, Chick!"

"Lady, I guess we better not go in here. Lady . . ." a small nervous hand plucked at her sleeve, but Nancy ignored it.

"*Chick!*" she called again.

He looked round, puzzled, saw her, and approached the door. "Good heavens, you have picked up some local color!" gazing down at the little group but making no move to open the grill. "Where on earth did you collect those?" For Chick, of course, was as familiar with Nancy's compositions as was the rest of the class. Nancy shifted her weight to the other foot and tilted her umbrella. It was raining harder now. "Open the door," she ordered. "Oh Chick, do stop teasing. I've got to come in, I tell you."

"Not with that gang." Chick was firm. "No. Nancy . . ." as Nancy pressed a small cold nose against the grill and shook it impotently. "No use displayin' your wimmin's wiles on me. I'm a hard boiled guy, I am. Got to be and hold the monitor's job," and Chick, waving a gay hand behind him turned and fled.

Nancy shifted her weight back to the right foot and cogitated. Gosh, what to do next!

But ah, who comes here? Elsie, bless his little heart! little 'E. Dinsmore,' nicknamed 'Elsie' by the class. Nancy pulled forth her dimple and displayed it alongside her most ravishing smile. Technique, this was, but all's fair in war and the illustrator's racket.

"Elsie . . ." she wailed. "*Do* hurry and let me in. It's simply pouring out here. . . . I've stood here and stood here and haven't been able to get anyone to let me in . . ." Which of course was the truth.

Elsie smiled obligingly and the door clicked open. "Gosh, you did get a whiffer! What's his name?" as the procession, obeying Nancy's imperious gesture pattered up the steps and began to drip in the hall.

"Oh, this is Willyum . . ." she indicated the puller-along. "And . . . ?"

"Billyum," volunteered the shover-ahead.

"And Ambrose."

"Ambrosia'd be better," commented Elsie,

sniffing. "The auditorium's empty. Better herd 'em in there. Hope the directors don't get a whiff of your models, they'll think a last year's still life has gone bad!" and dodging into the smoking room, evaded further responsibility.

The procession, dripping widely and somewhat overawed by the long, empty, echoing halls, filed silently towards the auditorium. Nancy herded them in and shut the door. They mustn't, she warned them, make any noise, but as they seemed too intimidated to do more than huddle in a bunch, she dodged out to get a larger sketch pad and hang up her raincoat. This, she thought triumphantly, was certainly the chance of a lifetime. And while she was out here she'd find a little food to keep Ambrose quiet.

Returning, she shooed the three onto the high platform at one end of the big room, played with lighting arrangements until she found what she wanted, then settled down to work. Ambrose, content with a large bunch of lettuce taken from the lunch room, seemed pleasantly subdued, and Nancy had stationed a boy at either end of the platform to keep him from roaming. There was a temporary difficulty about the height of the model, since an ordinary seat on the floor gave her only a view of his white undersides, scarcely the position she wanted. However a table was dragged up, a chair put on that, and Nancy climbed to the top. All was serene.

Once the model was startled and bolted to Billyums' end of the platform, but that was when Elsie, smiling in conspiracy, stuck his head in at the door.

Nancy violently waved him back. "You disturb the model," she chided him. "Keep out," then, "Hey, put a keep-out sign on the door, will you?" Elsie nodded, and the head withdrew.

Ambrose was easily gentled back into the pose and Nancy began another sketch. Goats, she learned, were difficult. They had sort of sticky-out hips, the cocky little tail was set rather far down, and the back legs were quite knock-kneed, like a donkey's. The head was abnormally long, perhaps the beard made it seem so, and the nostrils, set wide and high up, gave the face almost the appearance of a caricatured Irishman, long lipped and melancholy. Absorbed in her job, she was really beginning to get the hang of this goat anatomy; she had completely forgotten what time of day it was. Time, almost for lunch.

Now the lunch hour, at the Academy, is announced so that all may stop working, but especially so that the models may know when the morning's work is over. Not for another hour does the afternoon pose begin. Suddenly the air was shattered by a sound as of a fire engine in full cry. The big brass noonday gong, just outside the auditorium door had rung.

Ambrose stopped not for stream nor stayed not for stone. But with a flying leap, as that of a young frog or gazelle in first class condition, left that platform, looked wildly around for a split second, saw that behind that door came human and presumably friendly sounds, and butted forth. Nancy had forgotten that goats are such mountaineers.

It took her a moment or two longer to scramble down from her heights. Willyum and Billyum were slightly quicker. Hot on the trail of their goat they fled. Just as the doors of classrooms began to disgorge sculptors, stained with honest toil, wet clay and plastecene, portrait painters, snobbish in paint smeared smocks, little 'antiques' very grubby from charcoal dust, and Nancy's own illustrators. All clamorous for food, all bound for the basement lunch rooms. The long corridor was filling rapidly, its cocoa matting floor an ideal race track a block long and twelve feet wide. Ambrose took it at full speed, skidded at the end, wheeled with a patter of small hoofs on the bare stone, evaded the outstretched arms of a sculptor, dodged beneath the hold of another, and turned back, full tilt.

Cries of "What's that? Who brought that in?" Startled screams from the girls, the sound of overturned chairs, retreating footsteps as pupils crowded back to give the racer room. Ambrose, practically undeterred on the straightaway pelted past Nancy emerging from the auditorium. She had half a second to shove a chair in front of him.

Ambrose, worthy son of mountaineering ancestors, said "Poo!" to that and leaped it like a flea.

But the door at the end of the hall, the one that went out to the big stairway and the galleries, was fastened shut. Nancy thanked Providence for that. Ambrose, baffled, wheeled again. A group of giggling painters huddled in their doorway. He passed them at full speed. By this time Willyum and Billyum had formed a sort of fence, heading him off from the length of the corridor again. Ambrose wheeled, looked around. The illustration class halfdoor, open at the bottom, looked inviting. He could see legs moving about in there. He made for it, butted lustily, the doors parted, slapped shut behind him.

Well, at least they had him in a smaller place, if they could keep him there, thought Nancy, racing after the goat's worried owners.

Inside was what a yellow journal would have called 'a scene of indescribable confusion.' Eve was on a chair. "Just as though she saw a mouse," thought Nancy with a flash of amusement. Chick was brandishing a big backdrop drape, like a toreador's cloak, Cynthia had made a frantic grab for the goat's horn, but he shook her loose, skidded between two chairs, picked up, in passing a newly covered canvas and wearing it like an Elizabethan ruff about his neck, leaped for the model stand and the chair upon it. His sharp little hoofs beat a defiant tattoo.

"Throw it over him, throw the cloth, Chick!" shouted Nancy. Willyum was advancing slowly, muttering beneath his breath. "Ni . . . ice lil'l ol' goat. . . . Ni . . . ice ol' Ambrose!" Judy, almost hysterical with laughter, perched on the long magazine table and refused to join in so unsporting a competition. But Elsie, always on hand, grabbed the other end of the model drape, and together he and Chick launched it, like a fisherman's net, over the elevated Ambrose.

Chair, model stand, drawing boards, Elsie, Chick and goat collapsed in a cloud of dust.

They came up sneezing, untangled themselves to find Ambrose unharmed, but both Willyum and Billyum had hold of the string to his collar.

"How'd that beast get in here?" asked Chick, wrathfully smoothing back his disordered hair. Eve had descended from her pinnacle, looking as though she'd never even heard of goats or mice. Elsie was mopping his grinning face with a painty handkerchief.

"Please," Nancy, personification of meekness, volunteered. "I brought him in. Yes, I know Chick, you said I shouldn't, but honestly I had to have a model."

"Hey, what's this, a Navy football match, with mascot?" A sculptor stuck an inquiring head through the door. Just what was needed. The illustration bunch might disagree violently among themselves, but just let a painter or a sculptor suggest that anything was amiss and the class solidified in defence.

"Nothing wrong," said Chick coldly. "Just one of our models got scared at one of yours!" The door closed hastily. Chick couldn't very well resume his anger after that. "Well, all right," he turned to Nancy. "But take 'em out, right away. All of them."

Nancy was fumbling in her purse to pay the worried small boys. "It's all right, boys," she reassured them. "Take that home to your mother. And here, here's one for each of you. Thank you so much for coming. A whole shiny new fifty cent piece for each. And here . . . another. For Ambrose. Get him a new, strong collar."

It didn't matter, really, she told Chick, as Elsie took the boys and goat towards the back door. "I'd finished with the model. I think I know what a goat looks like now."

Friday morning, by means of a notice on the blackboard, the entire illustration class was invited to be the guest of Miss Brewster, for tea, round the corner at the Pewter Pitcher. As one man, one hungry man, whooping with hunger and high spirits, they accepted and at four o'clock, when the last pose was finished, jammed the little tea room to capacity. Elsie's stiff bristle brush head, Chick's fluffy blond mop, Cynthia's red beret, Eve's new spring bonnet, and a crowd more.

"Anything goes," cried Nancy springing on a chair. "If you don't like tea, get a chocolate malted and cake, or ice cream. The illustrations, you'll be glad to hear, are finished and went to the editor yesterday. This is my party, to celebrate."

Cynthia, grabbing her, pulled her down between herself and Judy. "We want you to know the illustration class is awfully proud of its baby. But honey, won't this set you back the whole price of the job?"

Nancy chuckled and pulled the two girls close to her. "Tell you a secret," she whispered, "this'll have to come out of my month's allowance," and Cynthia's shocked expression made her laugh. "The class has been so sweet . . . and they'll have a chance to help on the next. Got to keep 'em fed, or they won't help me on the next job."

"O . . . o. You're getting *another* story to do?" Cynthia was impressed.

"Mmmm." Nancy dipped her mouth to meet the long straw of her Chocolate Peppermint Soda. "Yes, in place of the last one. *That* has gone to my talented and respectful mama to do over. The editor," Nancy almost choked on her drink, "says I can do pretty girls, but he's darned if I know what a goat looks like."

CHAPTER VI

# *Follow That Car!*

NANCY ran a cobalt stained forefinger along the imposing row of art books; Michelangelo, Picasso, Matisse, El Greco . . . there was a boy that could paint! But most of these books were in mother's own library, nothing here in the public library to help on that Art Academy composition on Japanese perspective. The place where Japanese Prints generally lived gaped vacantly.

Oh well, there must be something in the encyclopedia; she could get that at home. She stood up, brushed the dust from the skirt of her new spring suit and picked up the two volumes of detective stories; the new Mr. Fortune, and the recent Lord Peter Whimsey, both of which she knew already, but they were compensation for not finding that heavy volume on Japanese Art. Passing out by the loan desk she paused to scan the detective shelves for a new title; but she knew them all. The astute M. Hercule Poiret, the subtle charming Peter Whimsey, the deceptively blundering, plaintive Mr. Fortune, even that granddaddy of all famous sleuths, Mr. Sherlock Holmes. No, nothing new today. Nancy turned towards the spring sunlight.

What fun to be a real detective, to meet one's criminal in the flesh and foil him, face to face! Heaps more exciting than the indoor life of a mere art student, to whom nothing ever happened, to whom each day's criticism from Mr. Henry, affectionately known as "Henry" by his pupils, was just like the last. "Goot! Goot! . . . It is goot! Continue, my child!" . . . and each week's model no whit more stimulating than the one of the week before or the week before that.

Nancy's artist mother would have diagnosed this as spring fever. But oh dear, how thrilling, this wonderful April day, when the smell of budding leaves swept smoke and carbon from city streets, to go quite mad and just mutter "Follow that Car" to an impressed taxi driver.

Oh, and how exciting it would be to . . . to lurk through a warm spring night, in a damp, dark culvert while, with palpitating heart, one waited for the villain to appear for the money, which of course would be hidden in the hollow tree! How marvelous to haunt the doorstep of "the house opposite" waiting for one's victim to emerge, not knowing whether he was armed or not . . . and to feel that Justice and Might and the Majesty of the Law were behind one, grateful for one's valued services!

Nancy, dawdling down the steps, was briskly jostled by someone who murmured an apology, a tall, lean man in a spring overcoat with a slouch hat pulled mysteriously over his eyes. The taxi at the curb swung open its door, the man popped in, gave a low order, Nancy caught a glimpse of a stuffed brief case on the seat beside him, the door slammed shut and the car rocketed off round the corner. Another taxi drew up in the rank.

Perhaps it *was* spring madness, perhaps it was boredom with that essay to be written, or maybe just a head full of detection and mystery, but all of a sudden a little wheel in Nancy's mind turned over, gave a click . . . and she leaped down the steps towards the waiting taxi.

"Follow that car!" The command rolled from her tongue as though she'd been saying it daily. "It's important." Her head bobbed towards the disappearing number plate.

The eyes of the dusky driver rolled a startled question. "What say, Missie?"

"Go *on!*" An impatient oxford rapped on the floor board. "Oh hurry, or you'll lose him."

The car slipped into gear. Down the long block from Worth to Minter street. For a moment the aged Stepin Fetchet in the front seat hesitated at the corner, then glimpsed the first car, a green taxi, rolling along Minter and put on speed.

"Dat de one, Missie?" he queried over his shoulder.

"Oh yes. But do hurry." Missie crouched on the edge of her seat, the madness in full possession now. Gosh but this was more fun than a movie, any day, this was being half a dozen detective stories all rolled into one! Then for just a moment sanity gripped her. What if she should catch up with the green car, what would she say to the man in it? Yet there seemed little danger of that; Stepin Fetchet's old ark wheezed and rattled . . . and a really good detective, Mr. Reggie Fortune for instance would be employing his time to better advantage than jittering on the edge of his seat. Oh yes, of course, one could note the hour and minute when the criminal . . . well anyway when the man left the library, and what streets he took to wherever he was going, and the number of the car.

Nancy glanced at her wrist watch and scrawled all this on a back page of the Whimsey book. She could copy it and rub that out later. Then the green car, numbered LL—44-28 turned left, struck Market Street and shot out past the Art Academy, past Park Square, and kept on.

"So don' you fret," crooned a bass accompaniment in the front seat. "We goin' to catch that old green taxi yet."

Park Square. And in another ten days the awnings and booths for the annual Flower Show would be going up in the spring sunlight. But Nancy wouldn't be there. First year art students weren't, this year, to be allowed to attend.

A new rule of the new director, Mr. Framingham. Nancy hadn't met him yet, but she knew he was a dreadful old fogey; anyone that would forbid the first year students to enter the annual sketching competition for the best painting of the Floral booths. His claim was that there wouldn't be room for all their easels, but if he knew the beginners class at all he'd know that only about six of them cared anything about it. But those six were good enough to compete with lots of the older students; well, that is, Eve Curtis and Sue James were, and Nancy knew she was pretty good, herself.

It was to be lovely this year too, a Dutch garden it was rumored, the flower sellers in peak eared lacy caps, with bright awning striped skirts, and gay aprons, just the background for the blowing glory of golden daffodils and the patchwork gaiety of stately tulips.

Far down the block, ahead of them, the green

taxi had halted before a store. Nancy leaned forward.

"Slide in behind the other car, will you? The man got out there."

"You wan' me to wait?" mumbled Mister Fetchet dubiously.

"Probably won't be more than a minute," Nancy reassured him, and followed the overcoated figure into the drug store. Purdies this was, the students came here for Hot Fudge Specials, but if she yanked her hat down over her eyes and slid quickly by the counter in best detective tradition no one would recognize her. She'd glimpsed the spring overcoat through the glass of a phone booth at the back of the store.

Easy to sidle into the empty booth next door, and the walls were thin. She took the receiver off the hook and appeared to be waiting for a number. Her throat was dry, her heart pounding so hard she was sure he could hear it.

Then clear through the metal partition, in masculine tones came the startling phrase. ". . . have the necessary plans right here with me now. We ought to be able to go full speed ahead with the plots as soon as you've looked them over."

Dramatic! It was almost melodramatic. Nancy could hear squeaks coming over the wire from the other end.

"Tomorrow is too late," continued the man in the overcoat. "We'll have to work together on this. One man alone can't handle him."

Nancy blinked, stood back to gaze at the wall an instant, then pressed closer. She hadn't, after all, bargained for a real crime. But this certainly looked as though she'd stumbled on something. What should she do? A Reggie Fortune or a Hercule Poiret would be able, of course, to remember every word of the conversation. Or else jot it down on his cuff. Lacking cuff, and being stronger on imagination than memory, Nancy, still pressing her ear to the partition, tried to wriggle round and get at her purse. The pencil and some paper was in that. But a shower of keys, compact, two bits of charcoal, a tube of Talens water color skittered along the floor of the booth. And the man was talking again!

"I've got the others tied up. Sanders was the only hitch and we can settle him tonight," it was saying.

"Settle him?" Did that mean "bump him off?" Gosh, it sounded like it! And with the others "tied up." And who was Sanders? . . . not . . . not *the* Mr. Sanders, treasurer of the Board of Directors for the Art Academy, president of the Downtown Commercial Bank?

Then they *must* be planning a bank robbery; Mr. Sanders was to be "settled" tonight, the others, whoever they were, were already tied up, bound and gagged in distant points of the city.

All this poured in a lightning, confusing stream through her head. The next remark seemed to seal any last doubts.

"That'll be your job, old man; to see to Sanders."

It was pretty obvious that the man was giving an order to one of his underlings. "And his back," Nancy wailed to herself, "had looked so like a gentleman!" But the bigger the crook, the better they dressed, or so the movies and the stories told one.

"I'll see," finished the voice, "that you get in contact with him around eight o'clock."

Nancy screwed round to peep at her watch. Four o'clock already! She'd have to get warning to Mr. Sanders. But she couldn't lose sight of this man either, till she knew where he lived, till she could identify him when she saw him again.

Next door the phone slammed into place, the

nickle tinkled into its box. Nancy, waiting for the man to pass through the store crouched against her instrument as though listening to someone on the other end. The front door of the shop wheezed shut, Nancy whipped out. The man was climbing into his taxi, her own still waited at the curb. Better let him get well away, but not too far. A good shadow never allowed himself . . . herself, to be seen.

But wait, wasn't there something she'd forgotten to do? No . . . o. She turned back, glanced into the booth that the man had used. Golly! There was his fat brief case, leaning against the back wall, just the sort of thing one would forget in a hurry. She darted in, grabbed it, was out to her own car before the green taxi had turned the corner.

Stepin Fetchet knew his routine by now. "Still a' followin'?"

"Oh yes," she was worrying about the brief

case. Should she look inside it? But she hadn't any gloves, and she might leave finger prints, or blur important ones already there. She hauled out a handkerchief, somewhat grimy with paint and charcoal, and wrapped it about the handle very gingerly, then sat back, pleased with that professional touch.

The cars slipped along the Loudinville Road. Ahead the red light flashed, Nancy rapped on the glass. "Better not get too close," she ordered.

"Yes," murmured Stepin meekly.

Lovely, that bed of crocuses glowing in the sun. For a moment Nancy Brewster artist crowded out N. Brewster, Hound of the Law. Oh, that lavender and smoky pale honey color, it fairly made one's fingers tingle for brush and canvas. Darn old Framingham anyway, who did he think he was, to shut out the first year students from the flower show! Perhaps if she could get together a delegation to see him, let him hear their side of it . . . but no, three or four students wouldn't make a very imposing delegation and the others didn't care enough.

The light changed, Nancy was yanked back onto her role. A big, west-bound bus swung ahead of them, out of a side street and lumbered to a stop to take on passengers. Stepin lost his place.

When the bus moved on and they shot ahead the Loudinville Road was empty of cars. Not a green taxi in sight, not even a yellow or a black. The road stretched, vacant, warm and pleasant, bordered by budding trees in the spring sunlight.

"Guess we done lose him, Missie," Stepin confirmed her worst fears.

What now did a Peter Whimsey do? How would Reggie Fortune handle this situation?

Oh, there was a green taxi coming out of Princess Street, where Henry lived. It looked

. . . surely it *was* the same taxi. "Wait. . . ," she shot at her driver, hopped out and sped across the road. A hand raised, the other car came to a stop.

"Taxi, Miss?" The face that leaned out was dark browed, heavy jawed, not pleasant, just the sort of driver that looked as though he were in with a criminal band.

"No . . . no. That is, oh please could you tell me where you left that man that just rode with you?"

"Hey, what is dis, de toid degree?" snarled the man. "Go roll yer hoop, girlie, I ain't in this game fer fun!" The gears rasped unpleasantly and he was off.

Nancy, holding the brief case with care, moved back to her faithful car. But . . . why hadn't she told the driver that she *must* find that man, that she had something of value belonging to him? And what would the astute

Hercule, the whimsical Peter, the resourceful Sherlock Holmes do in a case like this? Nancy shook her head. She only knew what N. Brewster, private investigations privately arrived at was going to do.

"Down the road to the left," she directed Stepin and at a small stucco house with a pretty green garden gate she got out. "Wait here," she told him. Here was Mr. Henry, head of the illustrators class for nearly thirty years, teacher to Nancy's own artist mother. She'd known him since she was knee high to a drawing board, and even the famous Mr. Holmes of Baker street sometimes took Doctor Watson into his confidence.

"Is Mr. Henry in?" she asked the ancient maid at the door. "Somebody with him? Well, I won't take long, but it's important, Mary," and holding the brief case as though it were dynamite she brushed past to the library door.

Mr. Henry, sweet and vague and pink cheeked above his immaculate white goatee rose from a chair by the window and, smiling, held up a warning hand. Somebody was telephoning at the desk, a man still clad in a spring overcoat, with hair slightly ruffled as though in agitation, and a voice that Nancy was sure she would always remember.

"But I tell you I must have left it there, I haven't been anywhere else!" insisted the voice at the phone. "Look in the phone booth . . . the *phone* booth, boy! Well, *both* phone booths. Well, go back and look again. . . ."

He glanced up then, saw Nancy, his mouth dropped open slightly as his eyes took in the brief case, and the phone was slammed back into its cradle.

"My case. . . !" He advanced towards her with one hand held out. This wasn't exactly the way a desperate man, a criminal, should act.

"Yes . . . s," she murmured and limply let him have it. But what was he doing here, the man that was planning to bump off Sanders, the Bank President? Oh dear, was Henry in danger too? He was such a sweet old innocent. But the man had the brief case open now, was spreading the contents on the table.

"These are what you'll have to get Sanders' O.K. on tonight," he was saying. "I'm leaving it to you. All the others have agreed."

"I don't think," said Henry, fingering his goatee, "that you've met Mr. Framingham . . . one of your . . . of my pupils, the talented Miss Nancy Brewster."

"Framingham! Ohmigosh!" breathed Nancy. The new director for the Art Academy, and a more harmless man never breathed . . . or . . . suspicion flickered an instant longer. Then her eyes fell on the plans "the papers" before him, and ruthlessly N. Brewster was shoved aside as Nancy, artist to her finger tips, charged across to the table.

Plans, in color. Plans for the Dutch garden show. All bright and full of spring, with little dutch figures standing beside little booths that subtly suggested windmills and Dutch doorways, but were not, after all, too odd and exotic for the quiet beauty of Park Square. "Oh, they're lovely. Who did them?"

Mr. Framingham looked up, grinning, pleased. "They are jolly, aren't they! Now if we can only tape old Sanders down to an agreement for the Dutch garden. He's got some fool idea about Venice in his head."

Nancy chuckled. "He's had that Venice idea every spring since Mother was in school. . . ."

Mr. Framingham looked puzzled. "I don't think," began Henry again, mildly, "that you quite caught the name. This is Nancy Brewster, but her mother is the famous Carol Heywood."

"Oh by Jove! Yes, yes. So Sanders has had that idea in his head for ages has he? Well, he's only treasurer of the Academy. If the rest of them have always been able to tie him up. . . ."

Nancy shuddered slightly.

" . . . why I guess we can."

"I'm sure you can." Nancy felt quite sure.

"But I haven't thanked you for bringing these back," he continued, all apologetic. "How on earth did you happen to find them? I was sure I hadn't left them at the library."

"Oh, I saw you leave a . . . that is the phone booth and followed you here." Nancy's spring madness was dying down, she felt like such an idiot. But perhaps even the great Sherlock made a mistake at times, one that his author didn't write about. The thought was consoling.

"So you brought them here. Quite right." Mr. Framingham began to shuffle the sketches together again. "I'll leave this to you, Henry. It's up to you to get your man."

Nancy longed to warn him that it was sort of dangerous to use quite such criminal language. It might get misunderstood some day. But perhaps he too read detective fiction.

He rose to go, apparently satisfied with that brief explanation. "You'll be at the flower show sketching of course? We'll expect something very fine of Carol Heywood's daughter."

Nancy shook her head. No, she couldn't be there. She was, you see, just a first year student.

Mr. Framingham looked aghast. Henry's expression was one of amusement. "But do you mean to say that that rule shuts you out?"

Nancy nodded. Yes indeed it did. And four or five others that were better than she was, she admitted modestly. Henry still looked amused. "I told you that wasn't a good rule."

"Well, if that's the case we'll have to wipe it out." Just like that. As easy as all that. Nancy protested mildly. "Well, perhaps it wasn't such a bad rule." Opposition, she had discovered a year or two ago, only makes some men more determined. It worked that way on Mr. Framingham.

"No more about it. I'll have it on the notice board tomorrow. Competition open to all students, first year included. You don't," he asked anxiously, "think it will crowd the gardens? Too many easels and whatnots?"

"Oh no. But he might have the first year group finish before noon."

"Yes, that was splendid. Splendid." And now he really must rush along. Henry would please look after those sketches. He said good-bye all around. "See you in jail. . . ," he shouted, smiling brightly. And zipped out.

Nancy sank into a chair. "Rather overwhelming, this Mr. Framingham."

Henry nodded, beaming. "And now tell me about it. I can see that there's more than meets the eye."

"Lots more," admitted Nancy ruefully. She supposed she'd better begin, she said, with the detective books. She glanced towards the door. Where on earth were they anyway? In the taxi? Oh my heavens . . . that taxi, ticking its little heart away.

For some moments a soft murmur had been going on in the hall outside. Now it resolved itself into Stepin Fetchet in mild expostulation with Mary. Nancy dashed out and hauled him in.

"I tells her I know you're honest," stoutly declared the loyal Stepin. "But I gotta have my *money!*"

Yes, but where was her purse? Not in the

taxi. Nancy having made sure of that dashed back. She'd certainly been a hot detective! Still, she had returned that brief case, even though the "plans" hadn't been just what she'd expected. Henry, bless his heart, had some change and bills in his hand, was paying off the grinning Stepin. So that was all right.

"But I think now," he suggested as the door closed again, "that you'd better stick to your own vocation my child. You had a nice drawing this week, imaginative, delicate, lovely. Imagination I may say is lost, even a deterrent, to a good detective. But for the artist . . . what are you phoning for?"

Nancy's giggle was apologetic. "I'm going to call Purdies Drug Store and see if that boy found a detective's purse on the phone booth floor!"

CHAPTER VII

# *Go West, Young Woman!*

OH DEAR, if that monkey would *only* keep still!—— Nancy scrawled a giant X through the sketch she had begun of him and scuttled along outside the big cage to catch him again as he swung perversely to the very topmost bar. Lots of other monkeys in the cage, almost a dozen, but somehow his small black wizened face, his air of disillusioned ennui had caught her the minute she entered the monkey house; it was his portrait she wanted and no other.

He made a flying leap across to a trapeze, nearly upset a smaller, mouse colored relative en route, and chattering shrilly, hung upside down for an instant. Beady eyes regarded

Nancy coldly as her pencil sped across the paper, then like a visiting fireman displaying his talents, the model slid across and down a rod, coming to rest in a far corner of the cage with his back squarely turned to his would-be portraitist.

Nancy said "Tcht!" laughed, and gave it up. If only she could get out west, in the far west, where there were lots of horses, lots of dogs, even lots of other animals, not just poor things shut up in Zoos or led on a leash, or standing guard with some policeman at a crowded corner. . . . Meanwhile she'd go draw elephants, camels, boa constrictors, lethargic creatures, or a stately lion.

Half an hour later, emerging from the lion house with a sheaf of quite nice sketches—the lions had appeared flattered at her attention—she collided with Ernestine Talmadge, also a member of the Academy Illustration class.

"Going or coming?" asked Nancy, cramming pencils into an overloaded purse.

"We . . ll, I was sort of sticking around." Ernestine ran crayon stained fingers through her dark bob, still further disordering that none too sleek coiffeur. "It seemed too nice a spring day to stay indoors."

Nancy agreed. A mild attack of spring fever, combined with irritation over this week's class model had sent her to the Zoo for the remainder of the morning. If you reported back at the Academy before you went home for the afternoon—and today was Saturday, it counted as a half day's work. Besides, ever since she'd sketched that goat for an illustration she'd felt that animals were even more fun to draw than humans.

"But lots harder," she agreed with Ernestine. "It's kind of a game to catch them when they're on the move. Sometimes you win, but," thinking of the monkey, "sometimes they do. Heavens! Half past eleven and I'm hungry enough to eat roast hippo! How about stopping at the first drug store counter, I want to stay downtown this afternoon, find a pet shop and sketch pussy cats."

As they swung onto the bus that would pass the Academy door, Ernestine had a better idea. They'd stop at the school, report for their morning's work, and then Nancy could come out to the studio she shared with her younger sister Pat. "It's Aunt Grace's studio really. She's a pianist you know. But you can draw our cat as much as you like, he's big and black and drapes well, and 'll stay for hours in most any position you put him."

Lucifer, his name was. Nancy fell in love with him on sight, and shedding hat and bag on a table piled with old magazines she hunched immediately over her sketch book, crooning to herself as one portrait after another of his Satanic Majesty rolled from her flying pencil. Behind a door at one end of the studio sounded the sizzle of bacon frying, the clink of dishes. It wasn't till Pat, a square untidy girl with a pugnacious nose and a twinkle, came out with plates and cups to set on the magazine loaded table, that Nancy emerged from her state of concentration.

Pat cleared the table by the simple process of dumping magazines, Nancy's hat and bag all on the floor where they immediately sank amid a sea of last Sunday's papers and the clutter of clippings such as all artists collect omnivorously. She tipped forward a small straight chair that held someone's skirt and gloves, they fell amid the clippings. Another chair was similarly cleared of two cushions and a dustpan, fortunately empty. And a third held a half full fudge pan and three books, besides Lucifer.

"Your model needs a rest," was Pat's apology; then she raised her voice, "Bring the silver when you come, Ernie!"

A scrabbled clattering in the kitchen. "Where are they?"

"In the tin marked Flour." Pat slid the plates to the now empty table top.

"No clean forks," reported the voice in the kitchen.

"Well, wash three then," and Pat grinned at Nancy. "Aunt Grace left two weeks ago. She had a short series of concerts out west and thought she'd run home after that, we live in Montana you know. But we seem to have been too busy to clean house since she left."

This did perhaps explain the condition of the studio, though Nancy refrained from comment. She didn't remember that the last time she was here there was that gray film of dust over chairs, tables, floor and pictures. Nor that the dust cover which Aunt Grace had wisely left over the piano top had been hidden beneath rolls of painters' canvas, a half dozen stretchers and the stretching tools. The couch was buried beneath a pile too miscellaneous to catalogue; a big lampshade, inverted, did duty as a fruit bowl, and beneath the piano were small piles of books and ornaments, unexplainable till one saw that the bookcase had been cleared and laid flat on its face for an improvised model stand. One of the window curtains served as drapery.

"My gosh, just *look* at this place!" Pat gazed suddenly around, as though, for the first time, seeing her home of the past two weeks. "Ernie, we haven't even cleared up after we had the model here last Sunday afternoon. We'll have to get busy tomorrow morning early."

"Not tomorrow, Lambie," Ernestine had arrived with the cocoa which she began to pour. "Elsie's got tickets for a concert. Next week, before Aunt Grace gets back. . . . Pass your cup, Nancy."

But Nancy, spying a small smear of butter mingling with the dust on the rim of her cup had slipped out to get another, or to wash that one. The small kitchen sink was almost too full of plates and saucers, pots and pans for her to reach the hot water. She ached just to roll up her sleeves and get to work, though it hardly seemed a one man job. How on earth did the place ever get into such a state?

Ernestine explained, "Well, you know how it is. At half past eight we close the door on all this, with a promise to give it a thorough clean up, once we're home. And when we get back at five we give a gasp of horror, and wonder how the place ever got so bad while we're away. Give Nancy some more scrambled eggs."

"Then it's a scramble to get supper," said Pat, "and be off again for the evening class."

Yes, of course, they were both working for the Temple scholarship, which meant three full classes a day.

"Then the last thing at night," said Ernestine, "we realize there's too much to tackle in our weakened condition, and plan to get up at crack of dawn to start the campaign. But Pat's always forgotten the soap, or the cleaning powder. . . ."

"Or Ernie hasn't wound the alarm," Pat took up the chorus. "And I'm beginning to believe," she added defensively, "that the place doesn't *want* to be cleaned! We'll get at it though before Aunt Grace returns. You going to the Surrealist show, Nancy?"

Nancy, pouring cocoa into the clean cup reflected that the studio itself was like a Surrealist painting, that oh-so-modern painting that was like the inside of an untidy mind.

Then the doorbell rang insistently.

As Pat flew to press the button that released the downstairs door, her paper napkin slid beneath the couch. Nancy's fascinated eyes followed it. "I'll bet," she told herself, "that Pat'll just airily go and get another napkin, and that one never *will* get dug out!"

All the same, they were grand girls, good artists and good fun. Ernestine like herself had found that her talent lay in drawing animals, she'd been brought up with horses and cattle and sheep on a big ranch out west. Nancy, whose summer travels with her family had been towards Europe, retained a regrettable vagueness concerning her own country. Cowboys, Indians, rattlesnakes, buffalo and horses all scrambled together in her mind when anyone said 'west of the Mississippi.' She fully recognized that gap in her own education and background, and had begged that this summer she might be allowed to go west alone, sketching as she went—an idea that had been promptly vetoed by both Dad and Mother. "It isn't as though you knew someone there whom you could visit, darling," was Mrs. Brewster's final word on the subject. There seemed nothing more to say.

A moment's delay, voices on the stairway, then Pat returning from the hall displayed a yellow envelope and a dismayed countenance.

"Patty! Anything wrong?" Ernestine scurried to meet her.

Pat gave one wild look around the studio, weakly flapped the telegram, and putting hand to forehead collapsed in a mock faint against the baseboard. "Read it to her Nancy," she gasped. "I ca . . . can't!"

Ernestine, snatching the wire, read it aloud. " 'On way, probably arrive tomorrow,' and it's signed 'Aunt Grace and. . . . O . . . . o, *Mother.*' Mother," she wailed. "My goodness, Pat!"

Pat nodded understanding, and as she scrambled limply to her feet explained to Nancy. "Mother's the kind that'll run her finger across the top of a picture to see if there's a speck of dust on it. I suppose that's why we've let things slide so, here. Home is simply spotless and it's been such a holiday, not to worry about dust and dishes and beds. But what on earth are we going to do now? You'll stay and help, won't you Nancy?"

Calmly Nancy cast overboard her program for the afternoon for the Surrealist show, and perhaps a Mickey Mouse. Of course she'd stay and help, of course she'd love to. But even the three of them, working full speed, could scarcely finish the job with any satisfaction. If only—her brain was beginning to whirl with a plan—if only there were three or four more, and a couple of good, husky boys. . . .

"I know," she cried, setting down her cup

with a click. And leaping to her feet she began immediately to take charge. "Ernestine, you go out and get soap, lots of it. And a new scrubbing brush . . . no, two of them, they're cheap. Have you got lots of clean cloths for windows?"

"Oh, I don't think we should tackle the windows," began the less sanguine Ernestine.

But Nancy had shoved her purse beneath her arm and started her towards the door. "Hurry, my chicken! Soap, scouring powder, brush . . . remember? Oh yes, and some ammonia," and closed the door behind her.

Pat, who had gone to reconnoiter the ground emerged from the bedroom to report that there'd be plenty of cleaning cloths, the last sheet had ripped clear down the middle; they could use that. But someone would have to go for the two weeks' laundry which was still down at the Chinaman's, they'd need clean towels, and linen for the beds, and table linen.

"Okay. Then you go do that. I've got an errand too, but I'll be back most as soon as you are. No, I'm not running away. Hunt out all your old smocks, we'll be needing them," and like an enigmatic whirlwind, Nancy departed.

The Academy. The Academy was the place to go for help. But who would still be there, after lunch on a sunny spring Saturday? She dived first for the big cool library, and hauled forth an indignant Cynthia from the study of fourteenth century stained glass.

"Need your help," gasped a breathless Nancy. "Come along while I find some others," and racing down the echoing, stone paved corridor, briefly explained. Cynthia's curls bobbed in agreement. Of course she'd help. Who else could they dig out?

Eve was run to earth in the dressing room where she had lingered overlong to admire her new spring hat. No, she wasn't dressed for any such stunt, she told them firmly. She'd planned to see a matinee this afternoon . . . and anyway it was too pleasant to stay indoors.

"A matinee is indoors," observed the ruthless Nancy. "We'll leave the windows open if you must have fresh air. May rain next Saturday . . . matinee then. Come on, Eve. Be a sport. You can borrow a smock from the line here, I shouldn't think most of these would look any different if you cleaned house in them," and she hauled a mouse colored garment from one of the laden pegs along the wall.

"No thank you," Eve shuddered and firmly replaced it on its hook. "I'll polish silver, or do something static, but I'll wear my own smock, if you don't mind. How about Chick now? He's somewhere around, mounting canvases in the basement I think." And having been hauled in to help she displayed an amusingly human desire to help capture the next victim.

Chick, grumbling that he couldn't see why the girls couldn't do their own job, and that he had work that must be done before Monday, was more difficult to hook. But Nancy declared he was indispensable. "And you can borrow an extra pail from Mike, the janitor. And a mop too. You're the only one of us he'd lend them to. Oh come along Chick, we've got to help those kids. But hurry, they'll think I've deserted by now."

For full measure she rounded up Harold who had remained to putter over a composition in the illustration room. Nancy voted it perfect as it was, but swore he'd spoil it if he worked on it any longer. And then Judy was caught sneaking out the big front door. Judy looked somewhat guilty, perhaps she'd overheard Nancy's conversation with Eve, but once captured she said she possessed a talent, hitherto unsuspected by her duller witted associates, for polishing glasses. "Lead on, MacDuff!"

It was quite a procession, armed with mops, pails and an extra broom borrowed from the suspicious Mike, that trailed through the warm spring sunshine back to the studio. The door swung open and Nancy heard Eve's first gasp of dismay at the job ahead of them. Cynthia called cheerily, "Here comes the cleaning brigade," to an agitated Ernestine, whose towel encased head was just emerging from beneath the couch.

"Oh bless you children!" cried Pat. "You're a whole bunch of life savers. Now who'll do what? I've got piles of soap, and it looks to me as though there was a broom for every one. I borrowed an extra from the people downstairs."

It was Harold's idea that they draw lots, but Chick vetoed the suggestion. "Plain loss of time." He was already stripping off his coat, rolling up his shirt sleeves, throwing open the wide windows. "I can lick my weight in window washers any day," and characteristically he was already at work before the others had even sorted out their respective talents.

Judy voted to do the dishes, then took one look at the kitchen sink and returned for Eve. "I'll need help here, it's a job for a dozen." Ernestine suggested that the kitchen shelves had better be scrubbed first, since most every dish was already in the sink, and volunteered to do it. Pat's job was polishing the piano. "Though who's been playing this with fudge and marmalade on his fingers, I dunno," she lamented as she began to sponge the keys.

The crowd, glad to stretch its collective muscles, dived violently into work, though it looked, thought Nancy, like a costume party gone mad. Piling pillows and ornaments out of the way she glanced up to see Harold's brush of black hair standing above the collar of his khaki painting coat as he wielded a dust mop down the long room. Chick, outside on the wide window ledge had twisted a red handkerchief round his forehead to keep an unruly forelock out of his eyes, and just a moment ago, as he had reached in for a clean cloth, Judy slyly stuck a long feather into the band at the back. Whistling, unconscious of his picturesqueness, he smeared white powder on the dusty panes. Eve had encased her red hair in a green bathing cap of Patsey's, and Cynthia, burrowing beneath the beds, had put on a pair of blue cotton slacks. Nancy's costume was a housecoat of faded cretonne, and Pat, strenuously polishing till even her face shone and glistened, had gone in for shorts and a polo shirt.

"We'll need floor wax, once we've got this swept." Nancy tossed another rug into the corner for Harold to shake, later, in the yard.

"There's a new can, here in the kitchen," called Judy. "Oh dear, what's your Lucifer doing? He seems to be stuck behind the ice-box."

"He's got a pet mousehole there," called Patsey. "Don't worry. Nothing ever comes out of it, but he's incurably optimistic."

Nancy, keeping time with duster along the baseboards as she followed Harold's broom, began to sing. Pat tapped an occasional note on the piano with her cleaning cloth, and through the window you could see Chick's gay head-dress bobbing in rhythm to the music. There was a long streak of white, like festive war paint, down his face.

"The duster goes down and a . . . round," she warbled lustily.

"And 'll come out he . . . . ere!" came the chorus from the kitchen.

"O . . . . o, o . . . o," was Chick's al fresco

addition. They were in full spate when the downstairs doorbell shrilled again.

"Heavens!" Pat's dismayed face, topped by a yellow duster appeared above the lid of the piano. "Hey, shut up, all of you. I left the downstairs door open, and if that's some of Aunt Grace's friends come to call. . . ."

Silence. Everyone stood as though frozen. You could hear your own heart thump. You could even hear footsteps on the stairs. One flight, two flights. Then the upstairs bell. Cynthia, tiptoeing in from the bedroom asked, in elaborate pantomime if she should answer it. Pat shook an emphatic head. All would have been well except. . . .

"Give me another rag, somebody," yelled Chick, throwing up the window and letting in a flood of spring breeze. He knew nothing of the bell, nor of Pat's decision not to answer it, nor of the dismay reigning within.

With a gesture of resignation Cynthia walked calmly across the floor, put her hand on the knob, then waved imperiously to Chick to shut his window, to the others to keep still. Nancy and Harold sank out of sight behind a huge armchair and Pat, stifling her giggles in the duster, crouched on the bench, the piano hiding her from the doorway. Silence in the kitchen. But since you couldn't hide Chick anyway, he closed the window and kept on polishing, his feather bobbing hysterically. Cynthia opened the door.

"Is Miss Talmadge at home?" Cultured tones that sounded like white kid gloves and calling cards. Nancy, shrinking as small as she could, hoped that a betraying foot didn't show beyond her chair.

"I don't rightly know, Miss. I ain't a seed her anywheres." Cynthia's accent was a weird hash of Cockney and the Emerald Isle. Behind her, Pat struggled with a snort, and Nancy was aware of rustling and a squeak in the kitchen. A white gloved hand appeared with a card. Cynthia accepted it with caution and a smudgy thumb. Her voice, Cynthia could always control her voice, demanded:

"Be this fer her, Miss?"

"Certainly," said the unseen visitor. Rather snootily, Nancy thought. Then, "Gerald, perhaps we'd better leave a note. We'll come in and write it!"

The studio held its breath. Suppose she did come in . . . and discovered a bedraggled art student beneath every chair. What on earth was Cynthia going to say? Suggest that the place was quarantined? That there was a mad dog loose in the kitchen? . . . That. . . .

"I don't think you really ought to, Miss. You in that nice frock and all," Cynthia's tone held only polite anxiety for the visitors. "Not till the exterminator man's come anyways. He's due shortly, Miss, but there's dreadful things underneath the furniture, I've seed 'em myself. As you might say, big as a yuman, just as I come in the door today!"

From the kitchen a slight crash, another squeak, a series of squeaks. Then calmly across the floor stalked the majestic Lucifer, and in his mouth a mouse. Mousehole sitting had won its reward.

He laid it, with the air of a hero bestowing his laurels at his lady's feet, beside Cynthia's sturdy oxfords. Cynthia never wavered. She just continued. "Ye see, Miss. . . ."

But the sound of departing visitors floated up from below. Cynthia firmly closed the door and raced to the window. "Chick, Chick! Come straight in here and remove this mouse. And Lucifer too!"

A hurricane seemed to have struck the

studio. "Almost yuman, am I!" demanded a mock-indignant Harold.

" 'Exterminator!' Oh Lor'. Aunt Grace'll never live this down," gasped Pat between shrieks of laughter. Nancy, limp on the floor, yelped incoherent delight. "Lucifer! . . . Oh, he . . . he looked so haughty with his mouse!"

From the kitchen emerged a scarlet faced Judy. "Eve's clear on top the stove; say's she won't come down till the mouse is out of the studio for sure. I swear, she made it from floor to stove top in one leap!"

Ernestine was patting the big black cat. "I'm going to muffle the upstairs doorbell with a sofa cushion, and go down and shut the street door, till we're through work. Next time Lucifer might miss his mouse."

Slowly the apartment was emerging from dust and disorder. The long floor, shining like dark water, with every rug meticulously in place, the bedroom with its neatly puffed pillows and fresh covers. Even the little kitchen was as fresh scrubbed as a drug store counter and Eve had polished taps and silver till they winked in the sunlight.

Nancy, with her head still in a towel, sank exhaustedly on the couch. "Feel as though I'd had a straight four sets of tennis," she mourned. "And how I'll ever get my hands back into shape, I dunno."

"Don't lean back against those pillows," Pat reminded her. Ernestine climbed up to remove the cushion that had muffled the doorbell and paused to gaze round her with pride. "Hope Pat and I don't have to live up to this standard. And I'm sure I don't know where we're going to sleep tonight, we'll never dare disturb anything or even walk across the floors. But we're terribly grateful," she hastened to add, with a brilliant smile all around.

almost too tired to think, even the picture of Chick, still in bandana, war paint and feather, scarcely made her smile.

What a dragon of a woman! Yet perhaps she hadn't been so bad. The upturned corners of her mouth, the little smiling wrinkles around her eyes . . . only the way she had stood there, in grim silence, as though she was making an inventory of the room. Then, as Nancy neared the Academy, her resentment began to dissolve in doubt. Perhaps there had really been something dreadfully wrong, perhaps, because everyone had been on separate jobs, something perfectly awful had been left, something they had all been blind to. Like . . . she almost giggled aloud—like Chick's bobbing feathered headdress. Yes, that must be it.

They swung in at the Academy door. A telephone was ringing in the front office, clattering away in the emptiness. Nancy waited, thinking. Of course the place was closed, but it might be something really urgent, a message for the caretaker. She glanced at Chick.

"Better take it," he nodded. "I'll wait." The pail clanked in his hand.

"Hello! This is the Art Academy, but the place is clo. . . ."

"And this is Ernestine!" A laugh at the other end. "And if that happens to be Nancy Brewster, let me tell you, child, that you nearly killed one of my two favorite parents. She's afraid she'll never get over the shock. Aunt Grace has taken her out to shop for groceries, and to get a malted milk to set her on her feet again."

It appeared that all the way east from Chicago Mother had been saying, "Grace, you were an idiot to leave my two untidy imps with your lovely studio." In fact Mrs. Talmadge had come east mainly for the purpose of setting things straight again and making good such articles as were stained, strayed or broken. Her worst fears had seemed more than realized when she had found her own two girls reinforced by half a dozen others. There should have been six times the mess, things should have been six times as bad. But they weren't.

"But what . . . what? I mean . . . oooh!" Nancy, hopping around like a goat on a tether was trying to listen with one ear at the phone, to still Chick with violent and to him, meaningless waggings of the face.

Aunt Grace had been triumphant. Mother, searching for dust, particularly in corners and along the mopboard, had continued to pursue verbal inquiries. And at last Ernestine broke down and admitted that Nancy was to blame for the whole scheme.

Then, it appeared, Ernestine's mother knew Mrs. Brewster, who, she said, was too capable a woman to be wasted on art. Ernestine swung into a fair imitation of her mother's brusque tones. " 'Wants to draw animals, does she, this precious friend of yours? I'll write Mrs. Brewster. I'll have every horse, dog, cat, sheep, cow, coyote, cottontail and jackrabbit dragged in from ten miles around. Maybe even a bear. Give her a fill of animal drawing. Put her off painting for life. Save the girl for somethin' better.' "

Chick, by now nearly frantic with curiosity edged still closer to the phone. "In the name of dynamic symmetry, what's that?" to the weird rumble that came from the ear piece.

"Wait, wait!" Nancy urged the voice on the phone. Then aside to Chick, "Hush, can't you? Sounds as though Ernestine's swallowed her tonsils."

Loud coughing on the line. Then Ernestine in her own character again. "Just between the two of us, old dear, Mother thinks no artistic eminence out of the reach of a girl who can dust in corners as you can. Listen, can you get hold of Chick? You're to come straight back, for dinner. Mother's promised us a two inch steak and all the fixin's, Cynthia and Judy have phoned home for permission, and I just dare you to refuse!"

Nancy set down the receiver, caught sight of something still nodding above the head of the unconscious Chick. "We're to dine with Ernie's Mother. Quite informal and all that. But just the same." Her voice began to slip, she caught the table to steady herself, collapsed, weak with laughter, into the nearest chair. "Oh Chick, I do think you ought to leave off the feathers. At least till she knows you better!"